BANSHEE, DEATH AND DISARRAY

HOLLY HARROW: A POINT MUSE COZY PARANORMAL MYSTERY BOOK ONE

KELLY ETHAN

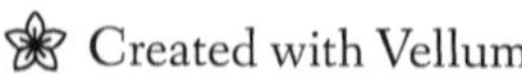 Created with Vellum

BANSHEE, DEATH AND DISARRAY

Death on vacation, blackmail, and the walking dead...let the mayhem begin.

Holly Harrow, witchy banshee, hates chaos and mayhem. Working at Elysian Fields Funeral Home satisfies her need for peace and serenity. The dead never talk back.

Until now.

The last thing she expects to find is an amnesiac man chained up in a coffin, scheduled for burial...

A live burial.

Now the dead won't stop walking and talking, and someone's out to kill her amnesiac charge. And for once, she can't blame her wicked witch grandmother, Elspeth Harrow.

Holly has no choice but to make a deal with death and track down a killer.

And don't even mention her talking, stuffed Viking raven...

ONE

"Just a quick trip, they said. No fuss." Holly Harrow, banshee witch hybrid and employee of the Elysian Fields Funeral Home, slammed her locker closed and stomped back into the marble-lined hallway. "Suddenly, it's a family emergency and they've hired a fill-in funeral director...and by the way, your vacation is cancelled."

Her twin bosses, Hector and Hillary, were descendants of the Greek ferryman, Charon. Normally, they'd give plenty of notice if they needed to take off on a buying trip for their obsessional love of death artifacts. Unfortunately, not this time. To make matters worse, the fill-in funeral director was Samuel *"Woo-Woo"* Wood. The man was obsessed with death and the supernatural.

"Don't you have a burial to complete, Ms. Harrow?" Samuel Wood loomed around a doorway near the prep and cool room, where bodies were stored before and after preparation for burial. A bushy gray, caterpillar-like eyebrow arched as he took in her casual attire. "I'm sure Hector and Hillary have a dress code for the funeral home."

Holly ground her teeth. Seeking calm, she forced a smile on her face. "Smart, business-like clothing, but since I was on vacation leave, and in town when my bosses contacted me, you get me as I am. Next time I'll dress in the correct attire." Creepy Samuel would just have to put up with it or she'd sic Elspeth Harrow, the wicked witch of Point Muse, on him.

Samuel made a non-committal sound, then sniffed. "If that's how the funeral home is run, so be it. Of course, if *I* was permanently in charge, things would be different."

And thank Hecate he was just a fill-in. His skinny, lurking persona made Holly binge eat her way through Cousin Lila's bakery. The funeral director looked like he belonged in a Dickensian novel. He wore Victorian style shoes and matching black trousers, a waistcoat with a hint of purple piping, and a top hat. *And* he smelled musty, like mildew and mothballs.

He flicked a finger at Holly's shoulder. "May I ask if that's regulation?"

Holly fought a wince. She'd already been in town with her cursed raven, Harrold, aka Harry, when her bosses cancelled her leave. She'd wanted to leave him with Lila, but he'd insisted on accompanying her. She hadn't realized Samuel had already arrived, otherwise she'd have ditched Harry. His whining drove her crazy on a good day, let alone while dealing with Samuel. She put her game face on and smiled sweetly, blinking her amber eyes innocently. "Harry? He's my familiar, and of course, you know that federal law allows me to take him to my place of work."

"Of course I'm aware," Samuel replied testily. "What I'm inquiring about is the fact he seems to have solidified on your shoulder. I'm certain federal statutes mention regulations for the treatment of familiars."

Did he just accuse her of familiar abuse? Red heat flushed from the tip of her flat, ballerina shoes, up her jeans-clad legs and onto her chest and throat. "I have never mistreated anything in my life. Harry is a cursed Viking stuck in the body of a raven, who has a nervous habit of turning into a stuffed taxidermy. Should we be talking about the fact he seems to do it a lot around you? Maybe he feels threatened by you?" She jutted her chin out. No fill-in funeral director with an obsession with taking over her job was getting the better of her. She was a Harrow, and they all came with claws and sarcasm.

"The nervous disposition of unusual familiars has nothing to do with me. Your employers have contracted me to make sure the funeral home runs smoothly while they're away. That's what I intend to do, whether people like it or not." Samuel smoothed the front of his waistcoat. "As to that, a last-minute burial has been arranged. No family or next of kin. The paperwork has all been signed off on. You just need to oversee the burial process. I have already notified your transfer crew. They should be ready to go."

Holly gritted her teeth. Her transfer crew consisted of Doug and Dave, twin troll brothers, and Leon, her gravedigger, and they were top notch, although Leon was a little more squirrely and less dependable than the twins. But then he'd only been working at the funeral home for the last few months. It was *her* job to brief the team about the day's schedule, not Samuel Wood's. Unfortunately, she didn't have a choice. He *was* her boss for the immediate future. "Fine. I'll go check the board and the mortuary register and get to it."

"As I said, the paperwork has been double checked, the register signed, and the board filled out. Our client is waiting for you graveside. Your crew has already set up the casket lowering system. Just do your job, Ms. Harrow. That's all that is needed." He checked his watch. "I have a business call to make, then will be consulting at an appointment in town. So, please don't disturb me for the interim." With a militarily precise nod, he spun and marched down the marble hallway to his office.

"Ghoul." Harry shook out his feathers and shuffled on Holly's shoulder.

In the daylight, Harry's feathers looked like they'd been lovingly oiled and shone in a magnificent kaleidoscope of black, blues, and greens when in the light. Not that she'd ever mention that, or she'd never hear the end of it.

His eyes, shiny balls of black, glittered when he winked at Holly. "I would watch him, banshee. He's after a permanent job here and you are in his sights. I don't think he considers a banshee as a reliable employee."

"He can try, but I think Hector and Hillary

would have something to say about it. If they ever get back from their family emergency."

"Maybe they have face-disfiguring boils and don't want to come back until their bulging, puss-filled, agonizing disfigurement has fled."

Shuddering, Holly poked at her pessimistic cursed raven. "They don't have boils. No one we know has boils. Quit with the boils. You're obsessed. I knew I shouldn't have let you stay up late watching all those witch infomercials."

Harry lifted his wings and zoomed around Holly's head, ruffling her smooth, brown, chin-length bob. "It was on the witch web. Boils are bad news. You need to take precautions, or you'll end up visiting a *volva,* an evil witch." The raven cawed, a sharp discordant noise in the silent hallway.

"I don't have blistery protuberances and the only witch I'd bother to see would be Elspeth, anyway. She's wicked but she *is* family." Holly grimaced. Of course, her grandmother would exact a penalty payment that would probably revolve around public humiliation. She touched the glands in her neck, just in case, and swallowed experimentally. No sore throat, so no infection and at this stage, nothing bulging. She was good to go. "No boils here. But we do have a burial. Let's just place a pause on the future possibility of bulging skin infections."

"Your funeral, little banshee." Harry clacked his beak in his version of a cackle.

"Eventually," Holly agreed. Poor Harrold aka Harry had been a hard drinking, rampaging Viking when he'd run afoul of a *volva*...a witch. The witch's lover had been part of the Viking crew, but he'd died. The witch, along with a native shaman, had killed the rest of the crew and imprisoned Harry in a dead raven's body, doomed to be stuffed when he wasn't attached to a witch as her familiar. The experience had given Harry a pessimistic view of the world. And that hadn't changed much since Holly had found him in New Orleans. "Right now, I need to make sure the paperwork is correct. Regardless of what Samuel says, I want to make sure there's no mistakes."

"Smart thinking, banshee. That one has conquering on his agenda. Best not to give him a reason to pillage your job."

Poking her tongue out at Samuel's closed door, Holly headed to the prep room.

"I'll wait out here." Harry shivered. "Dead people carry germs."

"You're a Viking cursed into the immortal body of a taxidermy bird. I think you're safe." Holly ignored her familiar's whining and stepped inside the prep room. The overall feel of the room was antiseptic and clinical, with a hospital table, aspirators, draining tubes, an embalming machine which sat in the center of the room, and a bank of refrigerated drawers that were built into one wall.

The medical grade stainless steel table had been steam cleaned and anti-bacterial cleanser used to make sure it was germ free, so the smell of sterile cleaning products hung strong in the air. The floor was polished linoleum, and the walls had the look of a hospital emergency ward. The room's white tiles were pristine and spotless, not a speck of dust in sight.

One half of the room, set up as a salon, had every imaginable color of nail polish, lipstick, eyeshadow, blush, and foundation. Even a stationary, pull down, old-school hairdryer stood waiting, ready for use. Not that Holly was involved in the body prep. That was strictly her bosses' and now Samuel's job. Holly ran the transfer and burial crew, and her boys were the best in the business.

"Speaking of work..." Holly turned to the white

board hanging on the wall closest to the door, with the open mortuary register on a desk underneath it. The white board listed the client's name, date of birth, method of burial, and date to be interred. Underneath, the register listed the same details as well as any personal effects found, other relevant paperwork, date of transfer, place of transfer, who transferred the body, and the staff member who checked the body in and signed off. Samuel's black, heavy scrawl marred the pristine white of the register. "At least he did that. It's just his high-handed maneuvering of my team I don't like." Holly ran her finger down the page until she came to the client's name. "John Doe." Not a name they saw often in their funeral home.

Poor guy. Imagine reaching the end of your life and no one knows your name. No one gathered at the side of your grave to say farewell. It was one of her ultimate nightmares...that and becoming one of the walking dead...or catching the plague...or... Holly wrenched her mind away from her tumbling dark thoughts and focused on the task at hand. She flipped through the paperwork, making sure everything was in order.

As she scanned the details, a note caught her eye.

John Doe's cause of death was listed as "natural caus-es," but his age was listed in the thirties. Surely it was strange for someone so young to die of natural causes? Holly frowned, wondering what could be so mysterious about this man's death that it distracted her from her work. She made a mental note to follow up on John Doe later, after the transfer was completed.

Closing the register, Holly turned to leave the room. As she did, a chill ran down her spine. She paused, looking back at the room, feeling as though someone watched her. She shook her head, chiding herself for being so superstitious. But as she made her way back to the hallway, Holly couldn't shake the feeling of unease that lingered.

Harry fluttered down to her shoulder as she walked. "You okay, banshee?" he asked, concern etched on his raven features.

"Yeah, just a weird feeling. Probably just my imagination," Holly said, trying to shrug off the unease.

Harry cocked his head, his beady eyes watching her closely. "If you feel like something's off, it prob-ably is. You're a banshee surrounded by death daily. You should trust your instincts."

Holly nodded, grateful for Harry's advice. Sometimes he made sense. As she walked down the hall-way, she still couldn't help but wonder what secrets lay hidden in the mysterious John Doe's death.

The skin of Holly's arms itched, and she bit her lip. Forcing herself not to scratch away like a mind-less creature, she clamped her arms to her side. The last thing she need was for her banshee gifts to act up while Samuel watched her like a hawk, but her gifts couldn't be denied. And something about John Doe was sparking alarm bells in her mind. She needed to find out more. Holly made her way back to the front office, where Samuel waited.

He stood with his arms crossed, looking down his nose at her. "What took you so long? I told you the paperwork was in order. You should be graveside already," he demanded, his tone condescending and biting.

"Just making sure everything was correct," Holly said, trying to keep the irritation out of her voice. She handed him the paperwork for John Doe's transfer.

Samuel flipped through the pages. "Every-thing's in order as I said."

Holly nodded. "Don't you find the cause of death unusual for his age?"

Samuel scoffed. "It's not our concern."

"I was planning on looking into it further."

"There's no need. Just make sure the transfer goes smoothly and on schedule." He slapped the papers back into Holly's hand.

Holly clenched her jaw, a flash of anger pooled in her stomach like a heated puddle of *I-hate-Samuel* lava...*or indigestion*. Samuel was so focused on making money and sticking to the schedule, he didn't care about the people they were serving. "Of course," she said through gritted teeth. Regardless of what Samuel said, she couldn't help but let her mind wander to the possibilities of what could have caused John Doe's untimely demise. Could it have been prevented? Or was there something more sinister at play?

"Are you waiting for my permission?"

Samuel's voice broke into Holly's thoughts. She stiffened. "I'll get right to it." Holly headed to the loading bay, but the hearse had already left. Sighing, she trudged the short walk to the back of the funeral home, Harry remaining suspiciously quiet upon her shoulder.

As they arrived at the graveyard, Holly took a deep breath and tried to focus on the task at hand. They had a job to do, and she couldn't let her overactive imagination get in the way. She nodded at the twin trolls who made up the heavy muscle of her transfer crew. Dave and Doug were solid guys...literally.

The troll twins were identical, except one had on a red shirt and the other wore blue. Otherwise, they looked like living, breathing, granite boulders. Broad, nearly seven feet tall, with arms thicker than a bushel of tree trunks. A sprinkle of dark coarse hair graced their large bald heads, like small patches of moss growing on a boulder. But the guys were easy-going and loved working outside on the funeral grounds. They also didn't have a squeamish bone in their trollish bodies. Their sister, Merry, was a smaller, feminine version with long blonde hair and colorful painted nails and worked the front as a receptionist.

"Hey, boss. We're ready to go when you are." One of the twins rubbed the back of his neck. "Dave might have thrown out his back getting the casket loaded onto the CLS though. Feels heavier than normal."

Dave groaned theatrically and pointed at his twin brother Doug. "He refused to help. I might need time off.'

Snorting, Holly shook her head. "Good luck with that. *Woo-woo* Wood is in charge while the big bosses are away. We'll be lucky to have jobs by the end of the week as it is."

"I told you. The ghoul's in the mood for pillage and plunder." Harry took to the air and circled overhead. "And the funeral home is his target."

"Thanks for your input but our fill-in funeral director is a putz, not a Viking." Harry might very well be right, but Holly had to focus on what was right in front of her or go crazy. She clapped her hands. "Let's get our John Doe buried before Samuel decides to critique our burial technique."

"He's loaded into the CLS and ready to be lowered, boss. Just press the button."

Thank Hecate for our new Casket Lowering System. Her bosses had splurged on the hardware after the walking dead incident that involved a cursed cauldron at a dragon's funeral.

The CLS was a lowering system comprised of steel bracing and frame in a rectangle shape over the freshly dug grave and had curtains covering the frame, so the mourner didn't have to see the casket descending. It had straps to lower the coffin and the rate of descent was controlled by the operator, in this case, Holly. Decking also surrounded the open hole and minimized the chance of cave-ins. A concrete burial vault was inserted into the hole and then the casket was lowered inside. The whole system was easy to use and streamlined the burial business. "Right, if everyone is ready? Let's get this show on the road." Holly grabbed hold of a small lever on the end of the CLS and slowly eased it to the left. The casket jerked a little as the spools on the side of the system turned, lowering the casket at a controlled rate... *supposedly*. Instead, the casket jolted again and the gears ground to a halt with a crunch.

"Not. Now," Holly muttered through clenched teeth. She reversed the lever with a hard yank, and the casket rose at a faster pace. Once it had reached the top, she shoved the lever back the other way. The casket jerked and wobbled as one side of the CLS ripped away from its base with a grinding crunch of metal. "No," Holly wailed as the casket slid off the side and slammed into the ground. The hinges on the coffin cracked as they impacted, and a body tumbled out of the coffin onto the surrounding deck of the grave.

A man's casually dressed body...

A man's body wrapped in solid metal chains...

A man whose eyes were open...and blinking.

A man who groaned and tried to sit up...

"That's not a good sign." Dave backed away from

the body and crossed himself, muttering a prayer. His twin brother copied him.

"Walking dead. Walking dead," Harry screeched overhead and vacated the area as fast as his wings could carry him.

"I'm cursed." Holly sighed.

This is all my grandmother's fault... somehow.

TWO

"Aren't those chains a pretty accessory?" Elspeth Harrow, matriarch of the Harrow clan, wicked witch of Point Muse, and Holly's grandmother, tapped the silver chains binding John Doe. "I wonder if he'll tell me where he got them from."

Holly rubbed her forehead and regarded her chaos-loving grandmother. Samuel would blow his top hat if he spotted the Harrow witch at the funeral home. He thought Elspeth Harrow was a loose cannon. Holly eyed her grandmother's eclectic outfit. If she was honest, he wasn't wrong. Her grandmother had an obsession. A very expensive obsession that centered on wigs. Any color, any shape. If it sat on her head, she needed it. Her collection had grown so large their sentient Victorian home, Harrow House, had added a dressing room just for the collection. Add the wigs to Elspeth's enduring love of colorful velour jogging suits, and the picture added up to a mayhem loving, crazy witch. Today's sartorial elegance included neon purple braids down to her waist, blunt bangs, and a violet, camouflage-patterned jogging suit that she'd topped off with lavender-colored combat boots. "Could we just get these chains off? This is a lawsuit waiting to happen. At least Samuel's name is on the register and not mine."

Harry cawed from his perch on a crowded shelf in Holly's small office. "Two words. Walking dead. Who knows what germs he's carried from the grave."

"Firstly, that's more than two words, and secondly, he never made it to the grave." Holly narrowed her amber eyes on her germaphobe familiar. "If you can't be helpful, zip it. We need to deal with this before Samuel finds out. He really will fire me if he discovers this mix-up."

"The foul-up's name is John Doe?" Xandie, Holly's cousin, and the Librarian to the Supernatural Great Library of Alexandria, tapped the mortuary register. "Is that normal? To have a John Doe buried here?"

"We get the occasional John or Jane Doe, but it's

pretty rare. And I've never had a mistake like this happen." Holly grimaced and paced in front of the chained, unconscious man. Once they moved him into the funeral home he'd lapsed into oblivion again. Xandie had a knack for solving a mystery. Maybe her cousin could flex her sleuthing knowledge and fix this problem before Holly lost her job.

"At least he's alive. But we really need to unchain him and get that head wound healed." Xandie stepped closer and peered at the crusted head wound.

"No kidding. Give it a try," Harry encouraged Holly's cousin from the sideline.

Taking the raven at his word, Xandie tugged on a chain, but it refused to budge and only elicited a groan from the slumped-over man.

Harry cackled. "Everyone's tried to get those chains off except the banshee. Even the oh-so-capable wicked witch admitted defeat."

Three sets of identical amber eyes glared at the taxidermy bird. All Harrow women shared the same-colored eyes, part of their witchy DNA that ran through the family blood line. Along with varying lengths and shades of brown hair and a penchant for stumbling over a body or two.

Sighing, Holly stepped around Elspeth and

stood next to John Doe. "Fine. I'll try and undo the chain that two trolls, a witch, and a Librarian can't remove." Holly grabbed hold of the chain with both hands. A jolt of electricity ran from her fingertips straight through to her brain. She dropped her head back as an ice cream headache to rival all others attacked, and her vision tunneled down to a pinprick. Her inner banshee had finally decided to show up after disappearing for the last few months.

Images raced through her mind as her surroundings faded. A figure collapsed on the ground. Someone else leaned over the inert figure. A cloaked shadow loomed behind. A meaty sound of something heavy hitting flesh and the flash of metal chains... A feeling of satisfaction permeated the vision.

A sharp tap on Holly's cheek drew her from her inner vision. She clenched her hands on the chains again for a moment before the metal suddenly pooled at the man's feet. She lurched forward and grabbed John Doe as he groaned and listed to the side. "A little help here, please?"

Xandie leapt into action, balancing John Doe from the other side. "Sorry, your demon eyes threw us for a moment."

Bracing John Doe against her hip, Holly frowned. What kind of crazy was the family peddling now? "I had a banshee vision. You've seen that happen plenty of times."

"Silver eyes, yes. Black eyes, muttering about the chain, blood spilled, and death and disarray, not so much." Elspeth picked her teeth with a fuchsia-tipped nail. "Maybe there's demon blood in the family line somewhere. Demons are fantastic chaos magnets. Shame about that sulfurous smell and being damned, though."

"Put him back where you found him. Bad omens. Bad. Omens," Harry squawked and shuddered on his perch before stiffening and falling onto his side... A taxidermy doomsayer.

"That stuffed act of his gets old quickly. Unlike my gorgeous baby boy."

"Colin's a pug fixated on his stomach, won't stop talking about filling his stomach. Or its contents or lack thereof. And let's not even talk about his radioactive flatulence." Holly glared at her grandmother. "Fix John Doe before Samuel discovers him and calls Xandie's husband to arrest us for interfering with the body."

"Technically, he's not a body, since he's alive, but *whatever*." Elspeth rubbed her hands together before grabbing a bright pink saltshaker out of her pocket.

"Must you add salt to everything?" Seriously,

sometimes Holly wondered if it was time for Elspeth to visit the Eternal Rest Retirement Home, permanently.

"Oh, ye of little faith." Elspeth stepped forward and shook pink, glittering particles over John Doe's head wound.

Both Holly and Xandie peered at the man's head as the wound slowly closed.

John Doe's eyes fluttered open and he jerked against the cousins. "Did anyone get the license plate of the truck that hit me?"

Holly grabbed Xandie's arm and drew her cousin out of the way. No one knew the identity of the previously chained man. He could be a psychotic nemesis of Elspeth, for all they knew.

Elspeth ignored her granddaughters and pushed at the wound, eliciting a grunt from the man in front of her. "It's closed, but it took longer than normal. I wonder if that's caused by proximity with those chains." She poked John Doe's cheek. "Oi, head wound guy. How do you feel?"

The man coughed and winced, holding his head as he glared with hazel eyes at the trio of women. "I was hit on the head, wrapped in chains, and almost buried alive. Plus, I have a blinding headache."

"Interesting. My potion should have dealt with

that headache." Elspeth used a combat boot and nudged the metal at John Doe's feet. "I need to research the chains back at my creation cave. It's possible they interfered with my healing potion."

"Are you sure your potion wasn't a dud?" Her grandmother *was* the ultimate wicked witch of Point Muse, but she wasn't infallible, and her love of chaos and mayhem sometimes meant hexes, potions, and spells went awry.

Elspeth sniffed. "If that's how you feel, why don't you re-chain and re-bury your John Doe and I'll just toddle off home."

Xandie stepped between the squabbling women and held up a hand. "Let's focus on the problem at hand."

The trio turned and stared at the man in dirty jeans and a navy, long-sleeved top, with chains at his booted feet.

He arched a bushy black eyebrow and stared back. "As the aforementioned problem at hand, I refuse to be reburied alive. In fact, why don't we talk about the funeral home's liability for burying someone alive? Where are your checks and balances to stop this from happening?"

She could kiss her job goodbye if John Doe decided to sue the funeral home for malpractice.

Holly pasted a weak smile on her face and cleared her throat. "All paperwork was carried out correctly, in line with our funeral home practices." She grabbed a bundle of papers and held them out. "Both the whiteboard and our registry were filled out correctly. It's obvious the chain suppresses any sign of life. The funeral home can't be held accountable." Holly ground to a halt, waiting for John Doe to reply.

"You didn't think it strange a supposedly dead body was wrapped in chains when it was placed into a coffin?" He took the papers and flicked through them. "John Doe? That's not my... I mean, my name is..." He stopped and closed his eyes for a moment.

Elspeth nodded wisely. "I thought this might happen when the wound closed so slowly. His brain is addled. It'll right itself eventually... *Or it won't.*" Elspeth shrugged. "Whatever happens, I want those chains." She narrowed her gaze on the occupants of the room. "Got it?"

John Doe shoved the chains over to Elspeth with a booted foot. "Have at it. On one condition."

"Yes?" Elspeth drew the one word out.

"Find out what happened to me. Until then, I'm glued to your sides... All of you." He nodded at Holly. "And my name is Nate." He rubbed his forehead. "At least, I'm pretty sure it is. It fits better than John does."

Poor guy. Whatever happened to him, he definitely hadn't asked to be chained and almost buried alive. Holly stuffed her sympathy down deep. She needed to protect the funeral home, not sympathize with a possible litigator. Even if said litigator had long black hair that lay in a tangled mess at the nape of his neck and dark scruffy whiskers that covered his chin, muscled shoulders, but a tiny waist. Not to mention hazel eyes that even while bloodshot seemed warm and welcoming. Nope. She absolutely hadn't noticed at all.

Xandie coughed into a hand. "Lecher."

Holly's head shot up, and red flared over her pale cheeks. "Shut it, Library Girl."

"Maybe she has a fever. Probably caught something off the walking dead guy." Harry twitched his feathers, then righted himself on the shelf.

"I thought that was a stuffed bird? Is this some sort of spell? Hazing the newly unchained guy?" Nate frowned. "I'm not sure what I think about your priorities."

Gritting her teeth, Holly grabbed Harry and tucked him under her arm. "Harry is my familiar.

For your information, he is a valuable part of my team."

"You know what?" Elspeth snapped her fingers. "Since you so generously offered me your chains, how about you stay at my place? Harrow House has plenty of room. Holly lives there with her mother, as well." She winked at Nate. "That way, you can keep as close as you possibly can while Holly solves the mystery of how you nearly ended up suffocating to death in her funeral home's coffin. Isn't that a great idea?" She beamed and then hefted the chain onto one shoulder. "Now let's get this show on the road or I'll start charging for my time."

Harry wiggled madly under Holly's arm until she let him go. He gasped for air. "Would it kill you to wear perfume?"

Glaring future murderous intents at her Viking raven, Holly opened the hallway door and peered out. "You were an unwashed Viking, you'll survive. Coast is clear." She opened the door wider, and Harry lifted into the air.

"I washed once a year, I'll have you know. I was very pro-wash for a Viking." Sniffing his outrage, the raven zoomed out into the corridor.

Holly turned back, arms folded across her chest. "Harrow House is yours, Elspeth. I don't care who you invite to stay, but it doesn't mean I have to speak to him."

Xandie grimaced. "It kind of does. If you want to make sure the funeral home and your bosses aren't legally at fault. Best thing you can do is find out his identity and who chained him up, as soon as possible."

"And I get the chains. My pretty chains." Elspeth patted the metal. "Now, hoist your patooties and get moving."

There was no way to win an argument with Elspeth once she had her mind set on something. "Fine." Holly growled the word through her teeth and stepped to the side as Xandie helped Nate stand.

"Whoa." He wavered on his feet and grabbed at Holly to balance himself.

"If you're looking for an anchor, then you're out of luck." Elspeth cackled and stepped out into the hallway. The lights in the corridor flickered for a moment before settling back down. "Holly's a pipsqueak to your giant size."

"I'm five feet two and a half inches. Not a pipsqueak."

"And I'm six feet. At least I think I am?" Nate steadied himself, holding onto both Holly and

Xandie before releasing them. "I'm fine. Just a bit of a head spin."

"Great. Can we go now before my fill-in boss decides to fire me?" Holly jerked her head to the left. "Go straight up the hallway. Big glass exit doors. Can't miss them."

Elspeth strutted ahead of the others. The end of the chains scraped the floor behind her. "Seems like the funeral business is a popular one." She opened the exit doors and then paused; Nate close behind her.

Holly didn't have time for her grandmother's shenanigans. She placed her hands in the middle of Nate's warm back and pushed. He staggered through the open doors, bounced off Elspeth, and stumbled down a few steps. Xandie hovered close by in case he fell.

Harry zoomed overhead. "We've got an issue."

"Of course we do." When did anything ever go right for a Harrow? They called it Harrow bad luck. Holly called it the Elspeth effect. What could go wrong would go wrong as soon as the wicked witch was involved. "Tell me it's not another body."

"Technically not *another* body, since the first body, aka Nate, wasn't dead. This time it's just a body." Xandie grimaced. "Sorry. I couldn't help it."

"At least I didn't find you standing over this one." Police Chief Zach Braun, bear shifter and Xandie's husband, stepped to the bottom of the stairs. He ran his eyes over the group, lingering on Nate and his dirt-covered jeans and top. "Does anyone have anything to tell me?"

"I got a new pretty. Just my color." Elspeth beamed and jangled the chains at the shifter.

Zach pinched the bridge of his nose. "Do I want to know why the wicked witch has a set of chains wrapped around herself?"

"Now, sweetie." Xandie left Nate and slipped an arm around her husband's waist. "Why ask such a question, when you really don't want to know the answer?"

"True." He rubbed Xandie's back and eyed Nate. "Is this Elspeth's new boy toy? Has the old paladin boyfriend been replaced?"

"No," Holly yelled, then bit her lip. That had come out a little more strident than she'd meant.

"You know that Elspeth and Buchanan are on a break, and Nate is Elspeth's new lodger, sweetie." Xandie smirked at Holly, her amber eyes twinkling. The Librarian's shoulder-length, frizzy brown hair waved in the slight breeze.

"And the head wound?" He nodded at the blood

that had dried in a track from Nate's hairline down his neck.

"Once again, do you really want to know more, honey?"

"I have what looks like a dead heart attack victim in front of the funeral home, blood on the ground. No obvious sign of a wound, and the appearance of a struggle in the surrounding area. I'm pretty sure I need to know something."

Holly grabbed Nate's arm and dragged him down the stairs toward the police chief. "This is Nate. We found him stuffed in a coffin, bound in chains, with a head wound that Elspeth healed. He has amnesia, but if you need to speak to him, we'll be at Harrow House. Tootles." She frog marched Nate past her open-mouthed family, dodging the crowd that had gathered, and headed for her shining, silver moped. Holly slowed as she spotted the last member of her transfer crew, her gravedigger, Leon, standing to one side, staring at the police. He twitched every so often, his long gray hair tangled, and his hands shaking as he fixated on the scene. If only he'd obsess over work like a murder scene. Holly frowned as she spotted another guy, this one short, rotund, and balding. It wasn't unusual for a crowd to form around a crime scene, but the man paid little to no attention to the police. Instead, he stared at Leon, unblinking. Who stared at a gravedigger instead of a murder scene?

Pushing the weird encounter out of her head, Holly shoved a spare helmet at the now quiet Nate. She obviously needed to be assertive more often. Because that exit had been worthy of Elspeth Harrow. She'd pay for it later, but the look of shock on everyone's face as she told the police chief the truth, then strode off, had been worth it.

Now if she could just solve the mystery of who'd chained Nate as easily.

THREE

"My pretty," Elspeth crooned and adjusted the silver chain higher on her shoulder.

"Could you please stop stroking your chain in public? It's discombobulating." Holly forced her eyes away from the strangely hypnotic sight of Elspeth fondling the same chain that had bound a man into a coffin.

"We aren't in a public place. We're home." Elspeth sniffed. "Stop harshing my buzz, banshee."

"Technically, we're on the front porch," Xandie pointed out helpfully.

"Anyone could be spying. Volvas have enemies. The trees have eyes." Harry fluttered his wings and shuffled closer to Holly. "I feel a cold draft. I might need my earmuffs."

Nate stared at Harry. "Do stuffed ravens even have ears? I'm curious now."

Harry rotated his head and glared at the former John Doe. "I knew you'd be prejudiced against taxidermy. You have that look about you."

"Hey." Nate backed up a step. "I'm not prejudiced against anyone. Live and let live... So to speak."

"Memory loss remember?" Harry snapped his beak. "How do you know you're not prejudiced? Unless you're actually lying? Maybe you're cursed? Maybe you have the plague and that's why they chained you. Maybe..."

"Enough," Holly roared and raised a fist to bang on Harrow House's door. "Let us in before I open a can of banshee whoop on these idiots. You'll be a lonely house when they're all gone." The front door inched open with an ominous creak.

"Thanks, House." Holly patted the door frame, then stomped down the hallway to the kitchen, where delicious smells teased her senses. She collapsed onto a chair at the dining table.

"Just in time, dear. I've made blueberry lattice bars and mushroom and smoked salmon pie for lunch."

"Thank Hecate's empty stomach." There was a reason she lived at home, and it wasn't her grandmother's delightful conversation. Her mom, Winifred, Elspeth's youngest daughter, was the kitchen witch of the family. Anything to do with potions, lotions, candles, and cooking, her mom was the go-to Harrow. Of course, she enjoyed her own cooking a tad too much and sat on the curvy side of the Harrow scale. Whereas Holly was straight up-and-down. She sighed. No matter how much the banshee ate, she couldn't add a single digit of measurement to her tiny frame.

Winifred popped her head out of the kitchen and pushed a dyed, fire-engine red curl off her sweaty forehead. "Did I hear the others?"

Harry zoomed in and grabbed the back of the chair as his perch. "Elspeth, Xandie, and the freeloader."

Perking up, Winifred scooted out from the kitchen. "I do like visitors."

"How about one we found chained up in a coffin?" Holly muttered under her breath but relented as she saw Nate hovering in the doorway. "She doesn't bite much, but her cooking is amazing, so we put up with her. You might as well have a seat."

Winifred snorted. "Ignore my daughter. She gets grumpy. It's because she's a banshee and a spinster.

We've lost all romantic hope for her." Holly's mother fluttered her eyelashes. "Are you single, by any chance?"

Groaning, Holly thumped her head on the table. "I just told you we found him chained up in a coffin and you're trying to matchmake?"

"You need all the help you can get." Elspeth sashayed in, chains around her shoulders and a pudgy pug at her heels.

"Yeah, the other two kids have hooked up. It's your turn now. My dame needs grandkids to corrupt...*I mean enjoy*." Colin, Elspeth's talking pug minion, sauntered over to Winifred. "Hey, Winnie. You got my special ready to go?"

Winifred grimaced. "Blueberry whoopie pie isn't a balanced meal, but it's better than you eating seafood." Holly's mom ducked back into the kitchen and came out with a large tray filled with whoopie pies. "Please don't choke. My mother would not be impressed."

"Eh." Elspeth waved a hand at her pug.

"See? Volvas are heartless." Harry bobbed up and down on the back of the scarred wooden chair.

Narrowing her gaze, Elspeth extended a fuchsia-tipped nail and pointed at the mouthy Viking bird.

Squeaking, Harry solidified on the chair and slid off onto the floor with a bang.

Sighing at her family's antics, Holly stood, grabbed her raven, and placed him carefully on the table.

"Did you have to do that? You know he'll whine about you hexing him for hours now."

Elspeth gathered her chain around her and headed for the back door. "I know. I don't even have to actually hex him anymore. He does it to himself. It's hilarious." Elspeth cackled, and popping noises sounded from the kitchen.

"Oh no, my lattice bars." Winifred fluttered into the kitchen, curses echoing out.

"My work here is done. I'm heading to my cave to do some tests on my pretty chains." Elspeth jerked her head at Nate. "Explain the house to him. If he enters my wig room, blood will be shed, and it won't be mine. *Tata.*" She yodeled the last word and skipped as well as she could with a heavy metal chain around her.

Xandie shoved Nate toward a spare chair at the end of the table. "Welcome to the family. May the Gods have mercy on your sanity because we won't." She smoothed her frizzy brown hair. "Don't go near Elspeth's bedroom or her wig room if you value your life. She's territorial." Xandie beamed. "There you go. All explained. Now we can eat."

"Well, it won't be my blueberry lattice bars that you'll eat." Winifred slapped a burnt, blueberry-covered oven mitt on the bench. "That wicked witch exploded them all. The pie's safe, but it'll be a while yet before it's ready."

"Oh, man." Xandie slumped and tapped her short, buffed nails rhythmically on the table. "I was counting on those bars. I need a sugar hit."

"You get plenty of sugar hits from Lila." Lila was another Harrow cousin, who ran the Point Muse bakery. Holly nibbled on her nail and stared at Nate. Harrow House wasn't for the faint of heart, but he seemed to be coping with the family eccentricity so far.

Nate glanced around the room, confused. "Are there some sort of rules or regulations I need to follow while I stay here?"

"The only advice you need in Harrow House is to be polite. The house can get cranky, and the consequences aren't pretty sometimes." Holly kept staring at John Doe, aka Nate, with the dark, curly, way-too-appealing hair.

"Ooh. A guest. How opportune for you, dearest. I'll tell the house to set up a room." Winifred clapped and beamed. "I need to plan the menu and..." Her voice trailed off as she scuttled out of the room.

"The house?" Nate frowned.

Holly poked her tongue out at her cousin. "See, I told you a better explanation was needed."

"Don't grump at me. I'm not the one who found the dead-alive guy at work."

Counting to ten in her head, Holly turned to Nate. "We're witches. A female witch line that can trace its history in Point Muse back centuries. Harrow House has been in the same spot in different incarnations for a very long time. It's developed a personality and can do things like create new rooms or change the floorplan. It can also move things around when it's in a mood. So, be polite." The house rattled the floor under Holly's chair. She stamped her foot. "I'm just explaining things to the amnesiac man. Go easy, you might drive him to run shrieking out of the house. Then you'll have no one new to play with."

The rattling under Holly's chair subsided, and she smiled victoriously at Nate. "You just need to know how to talk to it, that's all."

"You get used to them, buddy." Colin poked a paw at the frozen raven. "Wake up. The witch is in her cave."

A ripple surged over the fallen bird, and Harry fluttered his wings to right himself. "That witch is a menace."

"You do it to yourself. You know that. Don't give her the satisfaction of reacting, and she'll get bored soon enough." Lila strode into the room and slapped a container of cupcakes on the table. "*Bare-your-soul* chocolate cupcakes. I thought it appropriate." Lila flipped a long, brown, curly lock of hair over her shoulder and winked at Nate. "I heard Holly found herself a live man at work. I had to come and check you out for myself."

Xandie choked on the cupcake she'd just taken a large bite out of.

Holly thumped Xandie on the back. "You wouldn't believe how many times people choke around us. Even Harrows themselves. It's an occupational hazard."

"I'm beginning to see that." Nate rubbed the back of his neck where his dark hair curled. "You said something about a room?"

Holly opened her mouth to reply, but Colin beat her and answered first.

"I'll give you the tour. Make sure you don't stray too close to my dame's lair." Colin shuddered, his pudgy pug body rippling. "No one wants to take on that dragon." He poked Harry in his feathered side. "You're coming with us, bird brain. You can earn your keep instead of whining about germs." Colin herded Harry out the door as Nate joined them.

Lila waited until the trio left hearing range and slid into a chair. "That curly hair and scruff on his face is distracting." The baker witch fanned herself. "Alas, I'm taken. As is our resident Librarian. I wonder what single spinster Harrow might take a fancy?" Lila winked.

Xandie giggled, recovered from her choking fit. "There's only one single Harrow who fits the bill. Unless Nate's into cougars, and then your mom's a shoo-in with her cooking skills."

"I'm not here to pick up. I just want to save my job and shut down any future litigation."

"And find out who hurt Nate and help him recover his memory, right?" Xandie prodded her cousin.

"Yessss." Holly hissed the word. "Could we please stop talking about his relative hotness and focus on the issue at hand?" She refused to think about his curly hair or what he'd look like without scruffy whiskers. *Refused.* She was the last single Harrow standing, ignoring her mother's dating status. And she refused to give Elspeth what she wanted...a herd of Harrow great-granddaughters.

Lila slapped the table. "Lay it all out for us then."

Peace at last from matchmaking, Harrow style. "My bosses were called away on a family emergency, so they cut my vacation short and recalled me. They organized for Samuel Wood to fill in as the funeral director and mortician. I turned up this morning, and he gave me the John Doe burial that he'd already signed off on. I tried to lower the casket, but our system locked, and Nate fell out, wrapped in chains. I called Elspeth when I realized he was alive. She turned up, healed his head, and dragged him and his chains back to Harrow House. The end."

"Uh-huh." Lila tapped her chin. "Anything else?"

"Only Holly's touch removed the chains, and she had a banshee vision. And we found Zach outside the funeral home. With a body," Xandie added.

Lila frowned. "No one else could release the chains? Weird. What did the vision show you?"

Holly rubbed her nose. She hated talking about her visions. Always made her feel like an outsider. The only one in the family with banshee gifts. Her father hadn't had enough time to make an impact with his banshee lessons before his banshee gifts bonded with another family and he had to leave. He now lived in Europe. They talked regularly; it'd been years since they'd seen each other.

"Holly?"

"Fine." Giving in to Lila's prodding, Holly dropped her gaze to the table as she recanted what she knew. "I saw a figure on the ground. It was dark, probably at night. Someone leaned over him. It felt like they were trying to help him. Someone cloaked came up behind the guy helping, and I saw a flash of silver and that's it. I did get a feeling someone was pleased with their handiwork." Holly spread her hands out. "That's all."

"Then there was Zach's body outside the front of the funeral home. The guy looks to have died of natural causes, but there was a scuffle around him as well as shed blood. That would fit in with Nate's head injury. He probably stopped to help the guy and got bopped on the head."

"Why wrap him in chains and dump him in a coffin? It's a weird way to dispose of a body. And Samuel signed off on the register. He might know more about the job." Holly grimaced like she'd bitten into a sour lemon. "I just have to be subtle when I interrogate him. He can't know about Nate, or my job is done for."

Xandie nodded. "We have Nate's first name, and he must've been visiting Point Muse. There's only a few places he could have been staying. I know for sure Hazel's bed and breakfast is closed. She's visiting her daughter in Portland. There's only Mayweather Inn or the bed and breakfast owned by Sissy Corey. We'll need to check them out."

"I can do that. At least I can get away from Elspeth and her chain obsession."

Colin wandered in, sniffing food. "Yeah. My girl's in love with her chain. All you can hear from her cave is cackling."

"Since when do you go near her cave? You're supposedly giving Nate a tour of the house." Holly searched, but both Harry and Nate failed to appear. A very bad feeling coiled in the pit of her stomach.

"Harry thought he'd show amnesia guy Elspeth's creation cave." Colin shrugged, then wandered into the kitchen.

"Elspeth's cave." Xandie's eyes widened.

"Harry suggested it." Lila slowly stood, her body stiff like a person going into shock.

"I'm cursed, aren't I?" Shoving her chair back, Holly raced for the back door, her cousins nipping at her heels. She slammed the door wide open and made a beeline for Elspeth's shed out back, a.k.a. her creation cave. Where every manner of evil was plotted and carried out. The wicked witch's lair that absolutely no one, including family, were invited into.

"I'll shrink your manhood to the size of a pea. Don't think I won't."

Elspeth threatening to hex someone was a very good sign that chaos and mayhem were ensuing. Holly increased her speed, trying to head off the manhood shrinking.

"Harry just offered a tour of your workshop. I wasn't stealing anything." Nate backed away from Elspeth, his hands held protectively over his private areas.

Harry lay on the ground, not far away, flat on his back, wings spread wide and cawing what sounded suspiciously like bellows of laughter.

"Harry! What did you do?" Holly stepped in front of Nate.

The cursed raven swallowed his raucous caws and sat up. "I've done nothing. I am an innocent Viking. A simple cursed warrior. That's all."

"You pillaged and were cursed because you wouldn't stand up for a friend who ended up dying. Plus, you suggested the tour of Elspeth's cave. I'll deal with you later." Holly turned back to her grandmother. "He wasn't stealing. Harry set him up. Stand down, witch. No manhood cursing allowed here right now. Save it for the villain."

"Especially if you want grandspawn to corrupt," Lila added with a wink.

"Great-grandspawn, but you have a point." Elspeth clasped her chain to her bony chest and eyed Nate. "His brain is squishy, but everything else works. How do you feel about banshee witch children?"

"I... I..." Nate shook his head, befuddled. "I'm still dealing with the cursed, pea-sized manhood. I have no clue how to answer that."

"Trust me. Don't even try." Her grandmother had a one-track mind. From cursing genitals straight to grandchildren. No wonder Holly couldn't get a date. Not that she wanted to settle down, of course, she corrected herself. She was perfectly happy being a spinster. "Elspeth? Have you found out anything about the chain yet?" Anything to distract her grandmother from matchmaking or manhood cursing.

Sniffing, Elspeth stroked the metal. "I have a few ideas, but I need to run more tests before I confirm anything. But I think the chain's probably Greek in origin. I just need more time."

"Great idea." Xandie grabbed Holly and Nate

and towed them a few steps away. "Why don't you go back to testing the chain. Nate and Holly can go question Rose Mayweather and Sissy Corey. Nate may have booked in with one of them."

"Smart thinking, Librarian. There's a reason you're my favorite."

"Suck-up," Lila coughed into her hand.

Elspeth ignored Lila's snark and pointed at Nate. "Stay out of my cave or it's curtain calls for your manhood." She took a step back into the shed and slammed the door shut with a decided bang.

"Quick, while she's distracted. Make a getaway." Xandie shoved the couple toward the front of Harrow House and Holly's silver moped. "In future, ignore sneaky Vikings and stay out of the wicked witch's lair. You'll stay healthy and intact that way."

Holly rolled her eyes. "Everyone's a comedian." *Maybe it's time to move out...*

FOUR

"Has anyone ever told you that you drive like one of your clients?" Nate removed his motorbike helmet and shook his black hair out of his face, wincing as he did so.

"Excuse me? My clients are dead."

"Exactly. They don't have any more time left to live. They don't care how long it takes to get from the funeral home to the grave."

Holly placed her helmet in the basket on the front of the moped, surprising a squeak from Harry as he shuffled over to make room. "Are you saying I drive too slowly?"

Nate pressed against Holly for a few seconds as he slid off the moped. The momentary pressure of hard muscles against her back caused a stampede of combat-boot-wearing, stomping elephants in the pit of her stomach. Swallowing, Holly focused on Nate's insulting words.

"Yes, Holly Harrow. You drive like a snail. I'm surprised you haven't been attacked by road rage consumed drivers yet."

"You criticize my banshee's driving? You, who she rescued from a suffocating true death? Where is your respect?" Harry squawked and lifted into the air. Flapping his wings at Nate's face, he drove him toward the bed-and-breakfast steps.

"Hey, calm the rampaging, fierce Viking." Nate held his hands up in surrender. "I am very grateful for my rescue. I need to know why it happened and who I am. I'm just frustrated."

"Don't take it out on the banshee." Harry landed on a white, peeling porch banister and shuffled until his claws gripped tight.

"Can I ask why you're squabbling in front of my house?"

A woman's sweet, syrupy tones delivered the harsh words with maximum impact. Holly slid off her moped and joined Nate in front of the stairs. "Hi, Sissy. Sorry about the disturbance. Not everyone approves of my driving."

Sissy grunted. "Those contraptions are death

traps anyway. Is there any reason you're at my door bickering?"

"We need some help. Could we come in?" Holly turned her most winning smile on the woman. But Sissy had already turned away and strode back inside, leaving her front door open.

"Do we take that as an invite?" Nate whispered.

"Unless you want her in a worse mood than she is now." Holly jerked her head. "Mush, minions."

"I am a Viking warrior. Never a minion."

"And I'm pretty sure I'm a leader, not a follower."

"You know? You're amnesia man. You could be a craven coward, ready to run." Harry lifted into the air before diving low at Nate's head, ruffling his curly hair.

"Shut it, you two. Or I'll ask Elspeth to do something about your squabbling permanently." Holly ignored the warring duo and stepped inside the bed-and-breakfast. Sissy a.k.a. Cecilia Corey had bought the old bed-and-breakfast a while ago but had done little else to it other than accept paying customers. The old Victorian house, judging by the white peeling paint outside, desperately needed an external facelift. Yet inside, the house gleamed, and the smell of lemon-scented cleaning products filled the air.

"You're in. Now what do you want?"

Sissy stood in the middle of the hallway with arms crossed over her apron-covered, plump chest. Her hair surrounded her head in a halo of snowy white waves. Two emerald-green hair rollers gripped the front of her head and matched her colorful cat's eyes glasses.

"Well?"

Sissy might look like Mrs. Claus, but she could give Elspeth a run for her money in the mean department. Holly pointed a finger at Nate. "He was in an accident and has amnesia. We're here to find out if he was booked in here to stay. Might give us a clue to his identity."

Sissy raised an eyebrow. "No one was booked in here for the last few weeks."

"Are you sure?" The only other choice was Rose Mayweather's inn, and she hated the Harrows.

"Since you don't believe my words, I'll get my register. Stay in the hallway."

"Man, she's as scary as Elspeth." Harry landed on Holly's shoulder and shuffled until he pressed up against her neck.

"Yeah. Looks like Mrs. Claus but acts like the

Grinch. It's a conundrum." Holly scratched the side of Harry's head. "Have a look around, Nate. See if anything looks familiar."

"Brave little banshee. Or stupid. Never step from the path. Didn't your Elspeth teach you your fairy-tales? Nothing good happens to those who stray." Harry lifted off Holly's shoulder and circled around her head before zooming back out to the porch.

"Coward," Nate whispered. *"What?"* Nate pretended to look innocent as Holly glared at him. He walked along the hallway and poked his head into the sitting room.

"Well? Any flashes? Images? Anything construc-tive we can use to identify you?"

Nate stepped back into the hallway as the clumping of heavy shoes on the wood floor echoed throughout the house. "Nothing sparked. The owner has a large collection of ancient swords and knives, but nothing that triggers a memory."

"Hecate's burst balls." Holly gnawed on her lip. She'd hope Nate would see something and he and his somewhat appealing curly hair would depart and leave Elspeth in her matchmaking dust.

"There. Told you so." Sissy marched up with a small red book open in her hand. She pointed at the blank white pages. "Gnomes booked in four weeks ago. Try that blonde, Aphrodite wannabe, Mayweather woman. She likes having nubile young men around her. She probably jumped at the booking." Sissy eyed Nate up and down. "Although, you might be borderline on the age."

"Excuse me?" Nate's low voice rumbled in the hallway.

Wincing, Holly linked an arm through Nate's and dragged him to the door. "Thanks for your help, Sissy. We'll hit up Rose next." Holly waved over her shoulder but didn't pause in her rush out the door. She shoved Nate down the porch stairs toward her moped.

"Why are we in such a rush?"

"I don't want you to insult nasty Mrs. Claus. We'll end up in a hex fight, and I'll have to grovel to Elspeth to end it." She shoved her spare helmet at Nate again. "And no one wants that. Now mush."

"You have to stop saying mush. It's weird. And also, Harrows are pushy."

"You better believe it, buddy." A quiet Harrow was never a good sign.

Harry landed in the moped's front basket and slapped the side of it. "Crack on, banshee. I have Rose Mayweather to terrify."

Holly rolled her eyes but followed his directive.

For some reason, Harry loved tormenting the inn owner. He froze every time she looked at him. It freaked Rose out. If he wasn't annoying her or squabbling with Nate, she was all for it. It might make Rose more talkative and get Nate his memory back... *I hope.*

"Bad pennies always turn up." Rose Mayweather, inn owner and a descendant of the Greek goddess Aphrodite, patted her blonde, bouffant hairstyle that listed to one side.

"Hey," Holly protested. "I'm the nice Harrow, remember?"

Rose snorted, ruining her nineteen fifties housewife image. She leaned on her reception desk, her frothy petticoats swishing around her. "You're just quieter. That's worse for a Harrow. Well...quieter except when you're whining about germs. That's worse than Elspeth's mayhem loving antics."

"I actively look after my health, that's not a crime." Scowling, Holly tapped her fingers on the heavy wooden desk. "Enough with the insults. We need information." Holly reached out her hand without looking and grabbed Nate's arm, yanking him forward. "I need to know if you've seen this guy before."

"I thought you were the spinster of the Harrow clan?"

Nate bit back a cough that sounded suspiciously like a giggle. He cleared his throat. "I'm just an acquaintance. I seem to have had an accident and am having trouble remembering details about myself, except my first name, Nate."

"Not something you see every day." Rose fluttered her eyelashes and let her eyes drift over Nate's lean, muscled body. "I'd certainly remember such a strapping young man like you. But I haven't seen you before."

Holly fake gagged. "Please, no flirting. It's against the Harrow code. I just need to know if Nate was booked in here at all."

Rose slipped a bright blue notebook out from underneath the top of her desk and ran a finger down a line of names. She nodded. "A Nate Mortis checked in two days ago. Although he didn't make the reservation himself."

Nate Mortis? Ominous sounding name if she ever heard one. "Who did make the reservation?"

"An older woman, I think. She didn't give her

name but sounded older. And she giggled a lot." Rose grimaced. "I hate the gigglers."

"Did she say anything else?" Nate stiffened next to Holly and flattened his hand on the reception desk.

Poor guy. As much as Holly didn't want to feel any sympathy for him, she couldn't help it. She knew how she'd feel if she lost her Harrow identity.

"Nope. Just that you needed to relax, and she booked for ten days. I didn't check you in, so one of my employees must have. But your stuff is in your room. That's all I know." Rose crossed her arms. "Now you can leave. I don't want any dead bodies found here today."

"I'm not my cousins." Holly forced herself to be polite. She needed Rose on her side if she wanted to search the room. "We really need to get into that room, Rose. Nate needs his stuff."

"Not without identification. Customer privacy is paramount at Mayweather Inn."

Holly wrinkled her nose and stared. "He's an amnesiac found in an accident. We're lucky he can remember his first name."

Rose slammed her registration book closed. "That's tough. No ID, no enter."

Time to get tough, Harrow style. Holly nodded.

"I'm sorry to hear that, Rose. But we need to get in there. I'll have to pull out the big guns." She snapped her fingers, and Harry hopped off her shoulder where he'd hidden and onto the reception desk. He stepped carefully toward the inn owner and cawed softly at her, snapping his beak a few times.

Eyes wide, Rose stepped back. "You wouldn't dare."

"Oh, I would." Holly beamed and raised her fingers, ready to snap them, a prearranged signal she'd already worked out with Harry.

He fluttered his wings, the draft causing Rose's old-fashioned dress to swish around her legs.

"Fine. Fine." Rose took a breath and grabbed a key from the glass cabinet on the wall next to her.

"Room twelve. Top of the stairs. If he isn't staying, he can collect his bags and leave the key on the desk. I have to make my money somehow. This way, I can rent the room out again." She dropped the key on the desk. "Take that crime against the natural world far away from me." Spinning, she stomped down the hallway, muttering to herself about the evils of Harrow witches.

Snatching up the key, Holly whistled as she headed upstairs, Harry and Nate close behind.

"I take it Ms. Mayweather has a bird phobia?"

Nate crowded in close behind Holly as she paused outside Nate's room.

Stepping to the side to avoid the hot press of Nate against her side, she cleared her throat. "Rose doesn't like the fact Harry's cursed, talks, and freezes whenever she looks at him. Makes for a good pressure tool when she won't do what we need her to." Holly inserted the key into the lock and eased the door open.

"Genius... And cold. Calculating."

"I'm a Harrow, and I've been taught by the best." Holly stepped inside the immaculate room. "Well, you definitely weren't a party animal. Have a wander and see if anything clicks."

Nate walked around the very clean room and paused over two bags that sat unopened on the floor. "I guess, I didn't have much time to unpack before the accident."

Harry hopped onto the bed. "That's if you are Nate Mortis. It could be any chained man who was almost buried alive at the local funeral home."

"Could you two stop? You're giving me a headache. There's only one way to know for sure." Holly knelt next to one of the bags and gingerly unzipped it. She squinted inside, then slid her hand in. Rifling through Nate's unmentionables wasn't at the top of her bucket list. Nothing ruined the male mystique more than stumbling across ratty underwear.

"Anything? Or do you just like touching my clothing?" Nate winked at Holly, hazel eyes gleaming.

Argh. Why did sarcasm look so good on him? Latching onto something hard, Holly drew it out, along with a plain pair of black boxers, and threw them at Nate. "How about that?"

He grabbed the boxers and held them up against himself. "They could be mine. The right size, at least."

Pinching the bridge of her nose, Holly closed her eyes on the image of a naked Nate clad in nothing but boxer shorts. "Can we focus, please?"

Dropping his underwear on Harry's head, Nate grabbed the other object Holly had thrown... *A wallet.*

"Who turned the lights off?" Harry complained, shaking himself until the boxers fell off. He shuddered, hopping as far away as he could from the offending underwear. "That's unsanitary and probably a biohazard. Someone needs to take my temperature asap."

"Firstly, you're a stuffed raven. You don't have a

temperature and I really need to limit your television viewing time. *Secondly...*" Holly pointed at the wallet. "Open the cursed thing, Nate, before I lose my last shred of sanity."

Obeying, Nate flipped the worn, brown, leather wallet open and pulled out a license and credit cards. "Nate Mortis." He held up the license. "I guess that's me."

The small photo on the license matched the man standing in front of her. Holly nodded. "Yeah, that's you, without the scruff on your chin. Any memories yet?"

Closing the wallet, Nate slipped it into his jeans and shoved the boxers back into his bag. "Nothing except a blinding headache right now."

"Let's get your bags back to Harrow House and look through them. You might get something from that."

"And I can decontaminate boxer cooties from my feathers," Harry added.

Hefting the bags up, Nate nodded at the door. "After you, Ms. Harrow."

Hecate rescue her from a gentleman. He'd never survive around Elspeth for long. Trudging down the stairs, Holly slapped the key on the deserted reception desk. "Keep an eye out for Rose." Without waiting for an answer, Holly slid around the desk and grabbed the registration book. Flipping it open, she spotted Nate's name and the notation next to it. "The room's been booked *and* paid for, not just booked like Rose mentioned. That sneaky Mayweather's already been paid for a ten day stay. If you check out, she can rent that room and make more money."

Nate shrugged and adjusted his bags. "I don't care. I just want to find out what happened to me."

It seemed he hadn't really been as worried about his name as much as what had happened to him? *Interesting shift, although understandable.* Holly turned her attention back to the registration book and the last note. "Nixxie Mortis made the booking. Ring a bell?"

Grunting, Nate shook his head carefully. "My head's ringing, does that count?"

"Maybe. Let's get back to Harrow House so we can search through your unmentionables. Elspeth will love it." Holly shoved the book back under the desk. She needed to up her game, otherwise Nate would end up a permanent fixture at Harrow House.

Elspeth Harrow, Harry, and Nate in close quarters is enough to test anyone's sanity.

FIVE

"Who'd have thought someone with such a grumpy face would love colorful underwear?" Harry fluttered overhead and dropped a pair of boxers covered in yellow bananas on top of Colin's head.

"Aw man. Could you not do flybys and drop underwear bombs? It ruins my appetite, and that says a lot." Colin took a large bite of his vanilla cupcake with cream cheese icing. He continued talking with a full mouth, and food shot everywhere. "Why are we wasting time over amnesia guy's unmentionables?"

"Say it. Don't spray it." Holly wiped the crumbs from her worn jeans. She wondered how many germs could live on the food Colin had just peppered her with. "And we're looking through

Nate's belongings to see if we can find any other clues to what happened to him, and it might spark his memory."

"Got ya." Colin shook himself. "Is it time for a food break yet?"

"You just ate." Nate poked Colin's stomach. "In fact, you look like you've had five meals today already. Plus, I don't think cake's the best food for you. Maybe Elspeth needs to put you on a healthy eating plan."

Colin reared back, his paws scrabbling on the floor. "Healthy eating plan? That's a diet. How dare you swear at me."

Harry swooped over their heads. "Told you. That man has bad vibes." He hovered over Nate and dropped something white that landed on Nate's arm.

"Harry! No," Holly wailed and covered her eyes. That was definitely a mood killer. She wanted to spend sexy time with Nate, and those banana boxers' kind of appealed to her Harrow sense of the absurd. Holly spread her fingers apart and peered through the gaps, waiting to see Nate's reaction.

Nate stared at the white blob on the back of his hand, then up at the chortling raven as he circled overhead. Raising a thin, black eyebrow, Nate stared at Harry as he touched the white liquid then licked it off his finger.

Colin dry-retched, all thoughts of dieting disintegrating.

Holly clapped a hand to her mouth. On second thought, who needed sexy time with banana covered boxers?

"Yum. I think I love cream cheese icing." Nate smirked at Holly. "Did you really think I'd taste it if it truly was cursed Viking bird poop?"

"Ooh." Colin shot forward and hoovered the rest of the icing off Nate's hand. "Icing is the best."

"What did we just talk about? No more icing for you."

"Evil icing hater." Colin growled low in his throat at Nate.

Harry cackled. "That's right. Evict the icing hater."

"Everyone just calm down." Holly massaged her forehead. There was only one thing that would make this worse...

"Who are we evicting? Are we voting someone out?" Elspeth stood framed in the doorway, her new chain accessory looped over her shoulders, and black smudges covered her face.

"My queen," Colin squeaked and wandered over

to her feet, collapsing with a pant. "That icing hater swore at me."

Elspeth squinted. "Which swear word?"

"Diet." Harry swooped down and landed on the bookcase.

Gasping, Elspeth placed a hand dramatically over her bony chest. "I knew you were a bad egg when you invaded my creation cave."

"He's a dog. A talking dog, but still a dog. He could do with a more balanced eating plan. No one wants to send him to the afterlife early. Plan ahead." Nate frowned at Elspeth. "As the pet owner, this should be a priority for you."

"Pet owner?" Elspeth hissed. "He is my baby. Not a pet. Maybe we should plan a healthy eating plan for you. Bread and gruel are right up your alley."

"Look what I have here for our newest resident. My prize-winning chocolate cake with fudge icing."

Winifred beamed as she hovered in the doorway next to Elspeth and extended the plate out. A luscious, thick, chocolate lovers' delight sat proud in the center of the serving platter. She faltered as Elspeth and Colin glared at her. "What have I done now?"

"He deserves nothing. *Nothing.* Do you hear

me?" Elspeth glared at her youngest daughter.

"Could we get back on track? The sooner we work out what happened to Nate, the quicker he's gone. Does that suit you, wicked witch?"

"Fine." Elspeth crossed her arms over her chest. "If you're interested, I've worked out the chains are definitely Greek by design. The work belongs to Hephaestus, the Greek God of blacksmiths."

Nate pulled his second bag closer and searched through a side pocket as he considered Elspeth's words. His curly, black hair drooped over his hazel eyes. "Why would a Greek god chain and bury me alive? And why in Point Muse?"

"I have no clue. I'm just telling you the facts." Elspeth sniffed.

"I have a question. Why was I the only one who could release Nate?" *Elspeth is far more powerful than I am.*

"Oh, I know that." Elspeth brightened. "It was cursed. Only one who has one foot in the living world and another in the underworld can break the chains. You're a banshee and you work in a funeral home. You fit the cursed requirements to a tee." Elspeth clapped her hands, bad mood forgotten. "I'm the Master of Research. The queen. I totally dominate."

"Yes, mother." Winifred rolled her eyes and placed the cake on a small side table next to the couch. "You definitely dominate."

Holly wrinkled her nose. "Nate has a point though. Why would a Greek god try to bury him alive?" Who else had Nate upset other than Elspeth, Harry, and Colin?

Elspeth snorted, ignoring Colin as he sidled toward the side table. "Somebody he put on a diet, and they objected strenuously?"

"I just think icing shouldn't be a dog's staple food."

"You swore at him. *Diet?* Diet is a bad word," Elspeth hissed.

"Bad man. Bad man." Harry cawed over their heads as he circled the room.

"Focus," Holly bellowed, then rubbed her temple where an icepick of pain stabbed into her head.

"Colin! No," Winifred wailed.

Everyone in the room focused on the pug as he balanced on the couch arm before accidentally sliding off face first into the chocolate cake.

"My baby. Grab him before he suffocates," Elspeth screeched and lunged forward, but Nate beat her by an inch and snatched the pug out of his chocolate prison. Nate plunged a finger down the pug's throat and yanked out an unchewed wad of cake.

Colin gagged and shuddered in Nate's hands.

"Let go, you pug hater." Elspeth yanked Colin out of Nate's hands and clasped him tight, chocolate smearing over her clothing.

"Couldn't breathe," Colin gasped out, sagging in Elspeth's arms. "He saved my life."

"It wasn't your time to go. And if you stay away from chocolate and icing, you'll have a lot longer left." Nate scowled at Elspeth. "You need to be more responsible."

"*Responsible?* Why you..."

"He saved Colin. Just let it go." Holly grabbed Nate's arm to tow him behind her, and her senses exploded. Her head dropped back, and darkness crowded over her, warm as a blanket. Images flitted across her vision like a movie. The sitting room and Harrow house dissolved away. Replaced by random pictures. A group of ravens clustered together, discordant caws filling the banshee's ears. Trailing shadows twisted around her like a dark path. Mellow, rich laughter filled the darkness, melding with the shadows, gathering them in close to Holly and wrapping around her in a tight cocoon.

"Holly? Are you okay?"

Nate's voice filtered into her vision, dissipating the shadows, and disturbing the ravens. She blinked a few times, disoriented. A warm weight behind her back had her snuggling in and closing her eyes again.

"That boy ain't a couch, girl."

Elspeth's grating tone shot Holly's eyes wide open. Elspeth and Winifred crouched next to her, and Harry cawed from his perch on the bookcase.

"She has a tumor. A brain tumor. I knew it. She'll be dead in a month."

"She doesn't have a brain tumor," Nate rumbled from behind Holly's back.

Nate was her comfy, warm couch? Turning, Holly risked a glance over her shoulder. Nate sat close beside her, his hazel eyes twinkling.

"Falling for me, banshee?"

"You wish, Nate Mortis." As a comeback, it sucked. But Holly honestly had nothing. All she could think of was warm muscles and banana covered boxers.

"Your eyes went demon black again. And you dropped like a log. Quick-hands there caught you. What did our man-seeking banshee see this time?" Elspeth quirked an eyebrow at her granddaughter.

Clearing her throat, Holly refused to look at

Nate as she stood. "Shadows, birds cawing, shadow trails, and a woman laughing."

Winifred shuddered. "Spooky. I don't know how you stand it, dearest." She grabbed her daughter in a tight hug and squeezed her.

Patting her mother on the back, Holly struggled to take a breath. Her mom really needed to stop lifting weights in the form of pots and pans. Winifred's biceps would be the death of her daughter. "Okay, Mom. I'm good. Suffocating, but good."

"Sorry, sweetie." Winifred brushed a kiss over her daughter's forehead before releasing her. "By the way, Lila requires your presence at the bakery. She wouldn't tell me why." Winifred looked worried for a moment.

"She's probably about to fall into a sugar coma and needs someone to rush her to the hospital before she succumbs to a tragic sugar related death." Harry fluttered to Holly's shoulder, shuffling until he could wrap a wing around her neck.

"Could we not talk about death for a few minutes?" Holly forced a smile and pointed at Nate, attempting to be as polite as a Harrow could be. "As I can't leave you at Harrow House without the Elspeth Apocalypse happening, you and I have a date with a moped and the bakery."

"Date?" Nate winked. "I can't be sure, but I think I like forward women ordering me onto dates."

"What? I didn't... I...*hate you*," Holly stuttered, red fire blazing into her pale cheeks. Ignoring everyone, Holly spun, dislodged Harry, and stomped for the front door. *Why are the good-looking ones so annoying?*

<hr>

"You saw birds and heard a woman laughing?" Lila dumped a plate of blueberry cakes in front of Holly. "That's creepy. Horror movie creepy."

Holly pushed the cakes toward Nate, who obligingly took three of them. "I've lost my appetite, between weird visions and Colin falling into chocolate cake, head-first."

"These are good." Nate took a large bite before swallowing, then stared at the cakes. "I mean, I don't have much of a memory, but I'm pretty sure these are the best I've ever tasted."

"Small praise from amnesia man." Holly snorted at her own joke, but no one shared her humor as they all stared at her, mouths open. "What? It was funny."

"More like a tad insensitive. That's normally

more of an Elspeth thing." Lila leaned against the counter near her cousin's table.

"An unkindness."

"Are you saying I'm unkind?" Holly glared at Xandie.

"No." Xandie shook her head. "That's what a group of ravens are called. An unkindness or rave, conspiracy, a treachery, even a flock. I personally like a conspiracy." She shrugged. "It's kind of cool."

Lila snorted. "Thank you, Librarian Meyers. I wouldn't have been able to sleep tonight without knowing that."

"Geez, did you rob Elspeth of her snark today?" Holly sniped at her cousin. Lila was the oldest of the three of them and the snark was normally spread equally through the Harrows. But for some reason, today it had Holly on edge. Something about Nate had her banshee side suspicious, and her eyes had never gone black before or during a vision. What was so different about Nate? "Whatever ravens are called, I didn't get a horror movie vibe. More welcoming, warm like family."

"Ravens, shadows, and a woman giggling doesn't give me feel good vibes, personally. Maybe Harry's right. Your banshee gifts are off because you caught some kind of bug." Lila shuddered. "You do spend time with dead people."

Nate swallowed a large mouthful of cake before weighing in on the subject. "She helps usher those who have passed into a new phase of being. I think that's an important job. Her gifts will grow with her. This could be one of those times."

Lila arched an eyebrow. "You're saying she's having a gift growth spurt, and we shouldn't worry?"

"Indeed. Banshees are the connection between the land of the dead and the living. They are a gift and a promise rolled into one. We should support and honor them. At least that's what I think." Nate's cheeks fired red under his scruffy whiskers.

"Should we get you pom-poms for your new job as Holly's cheerleader?" Lila let loose an amused chuckle. "I love that you feel strongly enough about Holly's gifts to lecture us."

"Death is important, and those who help smooth the transition should be respected." Nate had a serious expression on his face, which he ruined by taking an enormous bite of his cake and chomping noisily, distracting everyone from his words.

"Your erudite young friend has a point. Even one made with cake crumbs on his face." Samuel Woods, Holly's fill-in boss, stood next to their table. He sniffed as he looked Nate over. His skin paled as he focused on Nate's face. He spun around to face Holly, ignoring Nate. "May I ask why you are here at this place on a date, instead of at work? I'm sure we have more than enough jobs to keep you occupied."

Harry hopped out from underneath the table next to Nate, took one look at Samuel, and keeled over, in full taxidermy mode.

Nate nudged Harry with his foot and snickered.

"This is not a date. It's a family emergency." She pointed at Nate. "I had to pick my cousin up. He's just been released from maximum security prison. Done his time and all that. Now I need to assimilate him back into society." Holly smirked at Nate, who coughed at her words.

Samuel ran a finger around his starched collar and smoothed the brim of his top hat. "Well, I guess I can allow it this once. But you need to get back to the funeral home. A streamlined process, with employees giving a hundred and ten percent, is a necessity for a smooth, functioning, funeral home." He snapped his heels together and spun, leaving the bakery without placing an order.

"That man gives me the creeps." Xandie grimaced. "I keep imagining him as Jack the Ripper with that top hat."

Holly tapped her short nails on the table, staring at Samuel's back as he retreated quickly away from the bakery. "He turned up at the same time as Nate, and he wanted to rush the burial as well."

Nate frowned. "He doesn't seem familiar to me."

Holly snorted. "You have amnesia. Nothing's familiar."

"Hey, I'm not that bad. I may not remember how I ended up in that coffin, but I at least remember how to be a functioning member of society. Well, sort of."

Holly snorted again. "That's not going to help us much at this point. Anyway, I still think there's something weird about Samuel. He's obsessed with death and the supernatural. You were buried with ancient Greek chains and your last name is Mortis. I think we'll put Samuel at the top of our list."

Nodding, Xandie agreed. "I think you're right. He's just too creepy not to top a suspect list."

"Should creepiness be a factor on the list?" Nate reached for another mini cake.

Lila grabbed the plate of food from Nate. "You've had enough. My cakes don't taste so great regurgitated, plus, the way you're shoveling them in, I'm worried about you choking. You've had enough near-death experiences right now."

"You need to stow the food anyway and hotfoot

it to the hospital. They've got problems. Head to the morgue when you get there." Hester, Lila's brownie employee, slapped a note on the table. Hester had been with the Harrow family since she was young and had known the girls since they were babies. "And I ain't your secretary. Next time, I hang up, no messages taken." Sniffing, she adjusted her apron and stomped back into the kitchen.

Yanking the last blueberry mini cake off the serving plate, Holly stood with a sigh. "It'd better not be another chained body. I've reached my limit on freaky." Assuming Nate would follow, Holly picked up a still stuffed Harry and headed for the bakery door, almost running into two younger women coming in. Apologizing, Holly tried to sidestep at the same time they did. Taking a pace back, Holly swept a hand in front of her. "After you, ladies."

Giggling, the two young women, with varying lengths of black hair, shuffled inside.

Nate ducked his head and hunched his shoulders as he followed Holly outside to Main Street. She clambered on her moped and waited for Nate to latch an arm around her waist. She really needed to solve this mystery as soon as possible because she was way too comfortable with his arm around her...

SIX

"Does the police force here ever get a rest?" Nate pointed out the cruiser with flashing lights as they pulled into the hospital parking lot.

Holly shrugged as she slid off the moped. "It's Point Muse. They're pretty much a regular sight around town." Holly pointed out the open ambulance that still had lights flashing. "I'm more worried about the ambulance with a crowd of people around it."

"Maybe another dead body in chains has turned up and the cops are here to arrest you for crimes against fashion." Harry cawed discordant laughter from his favorite perch on Holly's shoulder.

Shoulder blades itching, Holly glanced around the lot. Everything seemed okay except for the gathering crowd near the ambulance. So, why did she feel unsettled? Like someone or something watched her every move. Holly squinted at a bank of shadows on the far side of the area, near a group of large trees. If she were a peeping Thomasina, that's where she'd set up a spying operation.

"Do you need to visit the eye doctor? You could be going blind with that squint." Harry whacked Holly on the side of the head with his wing. He peered at her. "You're not cross-eyed and they aren't bulging. Maybe it isn't a tumor."

"Why is everything a tumor? I don't have a tumor." Holly stopped squinting at the shadows. "I just had a weird feeling of being watched. That's all."

Harry nodded sagely. "Probably indigestion. Pepto will help with that."

"Or someone *was* watching us." Frowning, Nate glanced around. "I can't see anyone. But someone did try to bury me alive. Who knows who's watching us?"

"Currently, the Point Muse law enforcement." Deputy Liam Harrow, Holly's cousin, stood frowning, mouth pursed, and amber eyes narrowed.

With his close-cropped brown hair and large shoulders, he towered over Holly. Liam was the grandson of Elspeth's younger brother, Edgar. Up until recently, they'd maintained a hostile feud but had made up when Edgar had come to town with a murderous fiancée intent on bringing the Harrows to their knees. Both Edgar and his grandson had settled in Point Muse, and Liam, ex-military, and sometimes black ops sniper, had taken up the police chief's offer of working with the police. Unfortunately, he had the same protective streak as Zach and loomed over all the Harrow women, trying to protect them from Elspeth's own brand of chaos and mayhem.

"You think you're being watched?"

Holly shrugged, dislodging Harry from her shoulder. "I'm a Harrow and we're naturally suspicious. Also, it could be anyone with a grudge against the family. That number is legion."

"Or it could be related to your new John Doe beau." Liam waggled his eyebrows and smirked at his tiny cousin.

"Everyone's a matchmaker." Holly glared at the deputy. "Is there a reason the ambulance is camped out in the parking lot, instead of in front of the hospital?"

Liam rubbed his chin. "We tried getting hold of that Samuel guy you work for, but apparently he's on a callout."

"Yeah, a bakery callout. Well, you've got me instead. What's up with the ambulance?"

"You need to see for yourself." Liam shoved through the crowd, making a space for Holly next to the ambulance.

Exchanging a confused glance with Nate, Holly followed.

"I told you, I'm *fine*." A man with a tangled mess of overly dyed blond hair sat upright on a gurney in the ambulance, torn shirt hanging off him. "Look what you did to my shirt. Someone will pay for a replacement."

Holly turned, confused, to Liam. "What does a guy needing a new shirt have to do with me?"

"Guy doesn't look familiar to you? Either of you?"

Holly shook her head and turned to Nate. "You?"

Squinting, Nate lifted a hand to his head. "I think I might have seen him somewhere."

Liam nodded. "He was the DOA in front of the funeral home. Zach wanted him autopsied at the hospital. When the ambulance got as far as here, he scared the paramedics by sitting upright, complaining about his shirt."

"Sir, I'm sorry, but you have no pulse." One of the paramedics backed out of the ambulance. "Even for Point Muse, that's weird. At least he isn't hungering for human flesh, I guess." The paramedic shuddered.

Holly tapped the ambulance worker on the shoulder. "You said no pulse?"

"Correct. No pulse. We've checked and checked. He's technically dead, but he's walking and talking."

"No chomping for flesh, brains, or blood?" Nate stifled a chuckle.

"No biting. He appears normal except for being clinically dead." The paramedic shook his head. "It's like he died and got rebooted."

"Not dead. Do you hear me? Not. Dead." The patient caught Holly staring. "What this is, is a potential lawsuit. They were sending me for an autopsy while I'm clearly still alive. You're a witness."

Leaning into the ambulance, Holly projected calm into her voice. "I'm sure it's a simple mistake. The doctors at the hospital can sort this out."

"Yes, well, you seem to be the lone voice of reason." The patient subsided and wrapped his torn shirt around him.

"Can I ask you a question?"

"I'm a captive audience until they let me out of this vehicle. But sure, fire away."

"Do you remember anything before waking up in the ambulance?" *Or becoming a non-brain chomping walking dead, as the case may be.*

The man frowned. "I went for a walk. My doctor told me stress isn't good and fitness helps."

"Anything strange happen on that walk? See anyone out of place?" *Like maybe a Greek god with a chain looking for a victim to bury alive?*

"Not really. There were a lot of shadows. I decided to cut my walk short, but then my arm started to hurt." He rubbed his chest absentmindedly. "I think I blacked out. I heard a guy talking softly. Telling me he was there to help. Then there was a thump and something heavy landed next to me. I woke up in the ambulance next. That's all I remember."

"That's enough. Thank you for your help. I'm sure the doctors will help you out." Holly pulled back to Liam and Nate. "He's definitely walking and talking with no lust for meaty body parts. Sounds like he had a heart attack. It's like the paramedic said, the guy died and rebooted again, but his body doesn't realize it's dead yet."

"Did he tell you what happened?" Nate stared at the ambulance. "Does he remember anything?"

"Pain in his chest and a man's gentle voice telling him he was there to help. Then he heard a thump and something heavy landed next to him. After that, he woke in the ambulance."

"And you think that heavy thing was me?"

Holly nodded. "I think there's a good chance you went to help, and someone knocked you out, chained you up, and tried to bury you."

"Why? What's so important about this guy?" Liam jabbed a finger at Nate. "No offense, but how did Nate's attacker know the bald guy would have a heart attack and your guy would turn up?"

"Maybe Nate has a stalker. Maybe someone arranged for the man in the ambulance to have a heart attack? Or maybe someone just knew where to be at the right time." Holly chewed on a nail. "But that doesn't explain the walking dead issue."

Liam grimaced. "It's worse at the hospital. Zach's up there trying to coordinate. He'll want to speak to you."

"Highlight of my life. Speaking to law enforcement." Holly rolled her eyes.

"Hey," Liam protested.

She patted his cheek. "I'm a Harrow. We are born with a distrust of authority. We blame Elspeth's genes. For some reason, the law enforcement aversion missed you. But that's okay. We love you anyway, despite your faults."

"It's always Elspeth's fault." Liam winked and headed back to the ambulance.

"It wasn't an accident, was it?" Nate followed Holly as she strode through the car park.

"What gave it away? The chains or the buried alive thing?"

"I meant someone planned the attack. Planned to bury me. Who does that?"

"Your nemesis obviously." Now that they'd passed the crowd around the ambulance, the parking lot was fairly quiet. Except for the two men at the end of it having a heated discussion. Holly took notice as one of them just happened to be Leon, the gravedigger from the funeral home.

"You know what the price is."

"I can't afford it."

"You don't have much choice." The short, bald man looked around and spotted Holly. "You've got my number. Make a decision." He hurried off in the direction of the hospital.

Leon dropped his head. His long, gray hair lay in a tangled mess down his back, swaying as he mumbled to himself.

Holly strained to hear his words. She could only make out a few jumbled phrases in another language. She had no clue what it meant, but she made a mental note to run the words past Elspeth. "Everything okay, Leon?"

Jerking his head up, Leon cleared his throat. "I'm fine. He was just trying to sell me a big screen television. But his price is too high."

"Uh huh." Why didn't Holly believe him?

"I have to get going. I'm booked to do the hospital lawns." He forced a smile. "I'm expanding my business. Grave digging and landscaping." He nodded to Holly and carefully averted his eyes from Nate as he scurried off in the same direction as the other man.

"Can this day get any weirder?"

"Depends if you're dead or not." Harry circled over their heads. "There's a line-up outside the hospital."

"Doesn't mean they're all dead." Nate frowned. "Surely there can't be that many deaths a day in Point Muse?"

"Pretty sure a wooden spoon shoved through the eye might be a sign of impending death." Harry clacked his beak. "I'm not staying around this germ ridden hellhole. I'll be waiting in my basket on the moped." He banked to one side and took off back to Holly's moped.

Holly shared a look with Nate before heading toward the hospital entrance. Maybe the dead-alive, heart attack guy wasn't an isolated incident? "Excuse me?" Holly pushed through the line-up into the foyer of the Emergency department of Point Muse hospital. A battering ram of raised voices and wailing slammed into Holly, pushing her back. Forcing herself forward, she apologized as she bumped into people. "Sorry. Not dying here. Just visiting."

"We hope," Nate muttered as he used his shoulder to open a path for the banshee.

A harried nurse with flyaway brown hair strangled into a not-so-tidy bun and a clipboard clasped to her chest rushed at Holly. "Nature of injury and/or documented death?"

"We're not dead."

"No pulse equals dead." The nurse tapped the clipboard with a pen. "Any plagues, germs, or communicable diseases that I should know about?"

"Honestly, we aren't dead or sick. We're just here to see the doctor in charge of the morgue. We're from the Elysian Fields Funeral Home."

"Oh." The nurse finally looked up from her clipboard. "Sorry. It's a madhouse here. So many walking dead people. Have to triage the cases and we're already running out of room. It's like an epidemic of death *or not-death.*"

"I can tell." Body after body packed every hard, plastic chair in Emergency. People sat on the floor and any available flat space, and clustered groups of people leaned against a wall.

"If you're after the morgue, it's two levels down at the end of the corridor. Space is even worse down there."

Holly worked up a polite smile. "That's okay. I know where the morgue is. Thanks for your help."

Waving them off, the nurse scuttled over to another group of people.

"Death should be gentle and peaceful. This is disrespectful." Nate glowered at the crowd of people who shouted and wailed around them.

Holly slipped an arm around Nate's muscled, trim waist and guided him toward the stairs. "Come on, Mr. Grumpy. Let's go talk to the medical examiner. Hopefully it's quieter down at the morgue."

"It's just not right," Nate mumbled as he let Holly steer him down the stairs into a hallway filled with people.

"So much for a little peace and quiet." Holly dropped her arm from around Nate's waist, rubbing away the imprint of muscle that she absolutely didn't notice. The hallway was a minefield of bodies. People sitting on the floor, huddled under blankets. Holly even spotted the odd toe tag, still attached. "It's a good thing Harry didn't come in. All these dead people would have spun him into a manic germaphobe episode."

"It's enough to send me into our psych ward." An exhausted looking woman with spiky blonde hair paused in the morgue's doorway. "Nice to see someone alive. I'm hoping you have an answer for this atrocity."

"Hey, Dr. Avery." Holly motioned to her companion. "This is Nate. He's a consultant. Dr. Avery is our medical examiner."

She waved the couple in and nodded at the hovering Nate. "Let's talk in my office." She led the way through a warren of cold labs filled with people and into a small office. "Take a seat." The doctor slumped into her chair and sighed. "Tell me you know what's going on. Because the rest of us are stumped and overworked."

Holly hated to let the medical examiner down, but when it came down to it, she had no clue what was happening. "Sorry. This isn't something we've seen before. Classic walking dead, yes. But..." Holly waved a hand. "This isn't like that."

"I was hoping you wouldn't say that." The doctor sat up and tapped a pen on her desk. "This is what we know. People are dying. Generally the time is just long enough for a medical specialist to call it.

Then bam. The patient is up and talking." Avery shook her head. "But they're all still technically dead with no pulse. It does seem to only be nonviolent or accidental death, though. Anything violent like murder seems to be permanent. People are dying and no one's there to collect their souls and ferry them on."

"What's happening now is an abomination. People curse death and underestimate what an important part it plays in the cycle of life." Nate leaned against the wall and growled.

Amnesia guy was taking this whole subverting death thing pretty personally. And the doctor had a good point. No one collecting souls so that meant Death was AWOL. Holly bit her lip. How powerful did someone have to be to take out Death? And how was Nate connected? A cramping stew of bad feelings and banshee misgivings took hold in the pit of Holly's stomach.

"About time you showed your face here." Zach Braun, Xandie's husband, bear shifter, and the police chief of Point Muse, nodded at the doctor. "We're ready to move the patients across to the new ward. I just need a word with Ms. Harrow."

"About time." With a burst of energy, the medical

examiner jumped to her feet and scuttled out of the office.

"That lit a fire under her," Zach remarked. "We've organized a ward for the dead-alive patients. It's just taken a while to get it up and running." He ran a hand through his shaggy, blond hair. "Let me guess. You've got nothing?"

Holly grimaced. "Not really. All I can work out is Death isn't taking the souls of people who die non-violent deaths." She snapped her fingers. "We can talk to Lila's boyfriend, Matthew. He's a reaper, so he might have more of an idea of what's going on. They're kind of death deputies. Surely, they know where Death is and why he isn't collecting souls?"

Braun nodded. "That's a good idea." He eyed Nate. "Still need your statement about your attack at the funeral home. I'll be out at Harrow House this evening to take it. Don't get into any trouble mean-while." He snorted, the noise reverberating in the small office. "Stupid comment. Forget I said it. Just try not to die." Zach walked off, chuckling under his breath.

He wasn't wrong. Trouble found the Harrows, no matter what. *Especially if your name is Elspeth...*

SEVEN

"What's next, Nancy Drew?" Nate deftly caught Holly as she nearly tripped over someone sitting in the corridor.

"Not ending up in Emergency would be a great start." She cursed her Harrow bad luck. At least she hadn't face planted this time, thanks to Nate's quick reflexes. Holly cleared her throat and stepped away from the warm temptation wrapped up in an amnesiac package. The last thing she needed to do was give Elspeth more ideas about matchmaking the spinster Harrow.

"What's the plan then?"

"Talk to Elspeth. See if she has any ideas. Plus, Lila's dad works for Hades, God of the Underworld. He might have some theories that could help us."

Nate grimaced, then rubbed his forehead.

"Is that pained look because of the mention of Elspeth or Hades?"

"Neither, I think. Just a headache is all. If Harry was here, he'd tell me it was a tumor."

"Don't encourage him." Her hypochondriac, germophobic raven thought everyone had a tumor. Holly felt the glands in her throat for a moment before forcing her hands away. Just because she was in a hospital didn't mean she'd catch something. Raised voices snagged Holly's attention, and using Nate's muscled shoulders as camouflage, she peeked around.

"Is there a reason you're playing peekaboo with my chest?"

If only. This close to Nate, the rumble of his voice in his chest rippled through her nervous system. Gritting her teeth, Holly focused on the couple arguing down the hallway. "No peekaboo here, but I just spotted that guy who argued with my gravedigger."

"And?"

"And now he's talking with a nurse I don't recognize. I'm interested."

"And the hiding?"

"He might see me. I want to know what they're

arguing about." But she needed to get closer. "Hold me," Holly demanded.

"What?" Nate's voice squeaked as he stared down at her, both eyebrows raised.

"Simmer down, Mortis. This is subterfuge, not an invitation. I want you to casually back up a few paces so I can listen in."

"And the hugging and touching?"

"Your body covers mine from view. Strictly business, no sexy time. Got it?" Holly glared at Nate. The things she did to solve a crime and keep her family off her back. She should get an award.

"You're the boss."

Nate's arms wrapped around Holly's back. She fought a shiver as a gentle band of muscle settled around her. *This might be a bad idea.*

"Operation shuffle commencing." Nate's voice mumbled above Holly as they slowly shifted back along the hallway wall.

Holly peeked around Nate. The man from the parking lot and the nurse still stood arguing. The nurse's hands moved sharply as she spoke. She certainly looked worked up as she poked the man's chest.

"Keep going," Holly hissed.

"Your wish is my command." Nate shuffled another three or four paces back.

Holly strained to hear the conversation, catching a few sentences now and then.

"That's his business."

"You need to tell Lover Boy to pay attention. Otherwise, the way this ends is on him."

"Don't you threaten us."

"It's not a threat but a promise."

That definitely sounded like a threat to her. Holly risked another peek.

The man stiffened and spun, spotting Holly and Nate. Placing his back to Holly's view, he muttered something to the blonde nurse, then scuttled off.

"Damn. He spotted me peeping."

"I take it cuddle time is done?"

Holly jerked her head up and snagged Nate's hard gaze. Warmth and humor stared back down at her. *Resist, resist, resist,* Holly chanted in her head. No way was she satisfying Elspeth's matchmaking needs. Clearing her throat, Holly pushed against Nate's chest until he dropped his arm. She wiped the feel of Nate's warm muscles off the palm of her hands. "He spotted me and bolted. But the nurse is still there."

"I sense an interrogation in our future."

Holly snorted. "I'm a Harrow. There's always an interrogation in our future." She hurried down the hallway before the nurse disappeared. "Are you okay? That look pretty heated. You should report him if he was hassling you."

The blonde-haired nurse twitched, then pasted a frosty smile on her face as she turned to Holly. "That's just Arnold Twigg. He's a janitor here. He has a cold and thought because he worked here, he could jump the queue to see the doctor. That's not happening."

"Okay." If that was all, why couldn't the nurse look Holly in the eyes? Holly squinted and read the nurse's name off her badge. "Callista? I haven't seen you around the hospital before."

The nurse trilled a high-pitched laugh. "In this crazy place? I'm not surprised. I've been here a couple months now. I guess that's why Arnold thinks he can get away with bullying me."

Holly looked the nurse over. From her artfully colored blonde hair and neutral nail polish to her expensive make-up, Callista screamed high mainte-nance rather than bullied victim. "Still, you probably need to speak to someone about him."

Callista waved Holly's words away. "Arnold's harmless. He just needs to learn to pick his times and if possible, make more friends than the creepy funeral director." The nurse grimaced.

"Funeral director? Name of Samuel, wears a Victorian top hat?" Holly frowned. Samuel supposedly only arrived in town just before he was due to pick up the fill-in director spot. So, why was he already firm friends with the janitor? He didn't strike her as a friendly social butterfly kinda guy.

"Honestly, I'm not sure if they are friends. I've just seen them together, whispering a few times. Although come to think of it? The last time I saw them together, they were arguing. And I saw the creepy top hat guy give Arnold an envelope after the fight. Maybe it was a sorry card." She shrugged. "Who knows."

And Holly had just seen the same guy arguing with Leon, another funeral home employee. Elspeth always said coincidences were for gullible idiots. "I saw the janitor arguing with a guy called Leon. He works out at the funeral home as well."

The smile dropped away from Callista's made-up face. "That's nothing to do with me. I need to get back to work. As you can see, we're extremely busy." She turned away and hurried along the hallway until she was out of sight.

"Something you said?" Nate stepped away from the wall he'd been leaning on.

"She clammed up when I mentioned Leon in the parking lot arguing with the janitor."

"The same guy the nurse was just talking to?"

"One and the same. Arnold Twigg gets around. Apparently, she saw Samuel, the fill-in funeral director, argue with the janitor and then hand over an envelope."

"Blackmail?"

"Sounds like it to me." But what had old Samuel been up to that had gotten him blackmailed? And what did it have to do with Leon and Nurse Callista? Holly hadn't realized she'd spoken aloud until Nate answered.

"Maybe Callista and Leon are dating?" Nate waggled his eyebrows. "I hear that's what normal people do when they like each other. Instead of going on frustration-induced moped trips to interrogate people."

Holly spluttered, nearly choking on her spit. Was this what flirting was like? Or was he just rattling her cage?

Nate patted Holly on the back. "Relax, banshee. When I ask you out on a date, you'll know." He winked at her. "I take it we're on a janitor hunt now?"

Holly forced her mind away from images of romantic meet ups without Elspeth lurking nearby and focused on a plan of action. "Let's hunt that janitor down and see what he has to say." Holly strolled in the same direction Nurse Callista had and slowed to a casual walk as she came across a nurse's station with a young woman seated at it. "Hi. Could you tell me where the janitor is? There's a truly horrible spill in Emergency."

The young nurse shuddered. "With the amount of body fluids being spilled currently in Emergency, I'm glad I'm not on the cleaning staff." The woman pointed to the end of the hallway. "The janitor's office is at the end of the corridor, just to the right. His door's marked. You can't miss it."

"Thanks heaps." Giving a wave, Holly waited for Nate to catch up. "The nurse said Twigg has an office just around the corner."

"We just have to make sure nobody sees us in there."

"It's not like breaking in, and I don't think they're worried about anyone searching the janitor's office. We'll just pretend we have a message for him." Holly rapped on the door labeled Janitor. After a few moments of silence, she tried the door handle, which turned under her hand and the door opened smoothly.

"We're not breaking in?" Nate crossed his arms, refusing to move nearer to the open door.

"Please." Holly snorted. "This isn't breaking and entering. That involves Elspeth and Great-Aunt Rose's skeleton key finger. This is just entering. If they leave the door unlocked, it's fair game." Holly poked Nate's chest. "You stay here as lookout. I'm going in."

"Why do I get the feeling we're about to see the inside of the Point Muse police station?" Nate grumbled but obeyed Holly and turned to face the hallway and anyone walking past.

"Because you're smart?" If he was truly smart, he'd avoid Elspeth. Her wicked witch grandmother seemed to seesaw between matchmaking and feuding with Amnesia Boy. Holly grimaced as she stepped inside the office. Arnold Twigg, to put it bluntly, was a pig...or someone had worked his office over. Paperwork lay scattered over his desk. Cleaning products sat tumbled on the floor on one side, and copious amounts of clothing and shoes overflowed a box, coating the floor in varying shades of color. "Who'd have thought the janitor would need his own cleaner?" Holly gingerly picked up a pencil and used it to move papers around Arnold's desk.

"Hurry up. I can hear someone coming," Nate whispered through the crack of the partially open door.

"Yeah, yeah. Hold your banana boxers." Flipping over a cleaning schedule, Holly unearthed a torn envelope with a ten-dollar bill sticking out of it. She used the pencil to draw the envelope closer and peeked inside. A collection of dollar bills was shoved inside. "Curious and curiouser." That nurse had mentioned seeing Samuel hand over an envelope to the janitor. Was this the same envelope? Why give a wad of money to the cleaner? Unless Arnold was blackmailing the funeral director. Arnold had argued with both the nurse and Leon, so maybe they were involved too. Blackmailers or the blackmailed? "Naughty, naughty Samuel. What have you been up to?"

Nate thumped on the door. "Incoming."

Pushing the envelope back and dropping the pencil on the desk, Holly scooted out of the office, just as another nurse paused in front of Nate. "Thanks for waiting, Nate. I just left a note for him."

"Arnold Twigg, our janitor?" The gray-haired nurse glanced suspiciously between the two. "I'm assuming you had a valid reason for being in his office?"

Holly tilted her chin and tried to mimic Elspeth's imperious indignation when questioned. "Of course. I've been playing phone tag with him about a potential opportunity. I was given his name by an employee of mine who's a friend. Leon?"

"Oh, the gardener. I've seen them together before with one of the new nurses, Callista." The nurse settled back, mollified. "Arnold's a character and hard to get hold of. He's gone home sick though."

Coincidence? Holly thought not. "Maybe I can get Leon to check on him? Make sure he's okay." Callista was involved, but on which side of the blackmail?

"Frankly, I'm surprised Arnold has friends at all. He isn't the nicest of men, but Leon and Callista are okay. They seem devoted to each other."

"Leon and Callista? I hadn't realized it was as serious as that between them."

The nurse rolled her eyes. "Leon's always popping into the wards to speak to her and they eat lunch together most days in the cafeteria."

"And Arnold? Do you see him with them a lot?" Nate addressed his questions with a thoughtful expression on his face.

"Not normally. I have seen them outside a couple of times arguing, and I know he approached Callista yesterday. He seemed worked up. Mind you, he has been quite erratic over the last week. Talking about an inheritance he's coming into." She rolled her eyes. "That's what Arnold's like. A bigmouth. Big plans that never come through. Yet his mother, Mabel, is lovely. A bit of a gossip but lovely. He still lives with her, but I think Mabel spends most of her time at Eternal Rest Retirement Home now."

"Goodness, I don't want to offer him a job if he's erratic. Thanks for your help, though." Holly nodded at the nurse and grabbed Nate's hand, hauling him along the hallway and outside to the parking lot. "I think we need to track Mr. Twigg down."

"You found something." Excitement gleamed in Nate's hazel eyes.

"I found an envelope stuffed with money. I think Twigg's been blackmailing Samuel and possibly Callista and Leon. Or maybe they're the blackmailers? I'm not too sure yet. That's why we need to speak to the janitor."

"About time. Have you disinfected yourselves? You can't be too sure what germs live in a hospital." Harry poked his feathered head out of the moped's basket.

Holly had forgotten all about hospital germs in her quest to track down Arnold. She slid her hand casually up her throat and felt her glands. No lumps. Looked like she'd escaped any contagious hospital diseases this time.

"Wow. At the hospital and no sneezing or whining about sickness. This must be a record." Lila sauntered up with her boyfriend, Matthew, in tow. She flipped her curly, long brown hair and winked at Nate. "Maybe you should stick around permanently. You might be good for our Harrow germophobes."

"That's Harry, not me. I'm perfectly fine. Just busy." Holly glared at her cousin.

"Don't get snarky with me. I come bearing reaper information." She pointed at her lurking reaper boyfriend.

"The man who was found outside the funeral home. His name appeared on a collection list. But the reaper who was assigned it said it just disappeared."

"That normal?"

Matthew shrugged. "Names will disappear when Thanatos pops up personally to take care of a soul collection. But it doesn't happen all that often."

Nate hissed and rubbed his forehead, squinting.

Holly shot Nate a worried glance. Maybe he needed to go home and rest instead of sleuthing.

"Thanatos is Death, right?" The sooner she got the information, the sooner she could send Nate back home with Lila and Matthew to rest.

"Personification of gentle death, non-violent death. His half-sisters, the Keres daimons, deal with violent deaths."

Lila curled her lip. "Yeah, those hags better stay away from me."

"Thanatos deputizes death to us reapers sometimes. We collect and then deliver the souls to his office in the underworld. Apparently, Hades is his godfather or something, so he hangs out there a lot. They're friends as well."

"But he does collect some deaths personally?" There was something there. A piece of important information. She just had to work it out.

"Sometimes. All non-violent deaths are his. He then shepherds the souls wherever they're supposed to go. But over the last twenty-four hours, names have appeared on our lists, then disappeared. Like the reaping isn't needed anymore."

That's it. "Or like Thanatos isn't around to collect or shepherd their souls anymore."

Matthew winced. "That wouldn't be good. The

souls would just rebound back into the bodies, even if those bodies aren't alive."

Holly snapped her fingers and pointed at the hospital. "Just like what's happening already. So, where's Thanatos?" She pursed her lips, a rough suspicion forming.

"I got my dad to call the head office. Apparently, Thanatos was in a meeting, but a secretary swore she'd seen him. She's been told there's a glitch in the system, but Thanatos is flat out trying to fix it."

Her suspicions bit the dust. Nate wasn't Thanatos after all if his secretary had seen him that morning. Nate hadn't left her side. He wasn't Thanatos.

"I have a lead on the janitor, Arnold Twigg. I'm going to interview him now. You guys can take Nate back to Harrow House for a rest."

"Poor little boy needs a rest. Let the warriors deal with the sleuthing." Harry clicked his beak at Nate, mocking him.

"Firstly, you're a stuffed, cursed bird, not a man, and Holly's a grown woman. And secondly, I'm fine. I'm not leaving your side until we work out what's going on. Funeral home liability. Remember?"

"Argh." Holly threw up her hands. She didn't

know whether to be pleased or concerned he'd noticed she was a grown woman.

Lila winked and grabbed Harry out of the moped and tucked him under her arm. "How about I take Mr. Germs with me. He can keep Nash company. That way you can both sleuth distraction free." She fluttered her eyelids at Nate,

"That was a surprise attack. I wasn't ready." Harry squirmed under Lila's arm. "Always with the armpits. Would it kill you Harrow women to wear deodorant?"

Lila grabbed Harry's beak tight so he couldn't talk. "You mentioned Twigg? I deliver cupcakes to his mom. They're out near the national park where Elspeth's witchshine stills are. An old falling down cottage. You can't miss it. Mabel, his mother, is nice but too old to live there without help and Arnold's a waste of space. She's just moved into the retirement home. Arnold's a gambler by the way, so he's always on the lookout for a get-rich-quick scheme."

"The type to blackmail someone?"

"Oh yeah." Lila nodded. "As dodgy as they come. Watch yourself, cuz." Lila hoisted Harry onto her shoulder and turned to head back to her bakery van. Before she'd taken more than a couple of steps,

Harry had lifted off her shoulder and flapped his way over to Holly.

"Hey, you need me," he cawed, then turned his head to snap his beak at Nate. "I need to be here so I can keep an eye on this rascally amnesia jerk."

Lila shrugged. "Suit yourself. Sorry, Holly, he's all yours." She retreated to her van.

Matthew lingered for a few moments. "I'll make sure Dad keeps on nagging Thanatos' secretary. And I'll update you if I get any information." He waved and followed Lila.

Holly eyed Nate. "You sure you're up for this?"

Nate grabbed his helmet. "I am ready for anything you can dish out, Holly 'not-a-speedster' Harrow."

"We'll see." Holly clambered onto her moped and gunned the engine before taking off at a slow snail's pace.

When you're a Harrow, there's a higher-than-average chance of something going wrong. I'm not going to increase my chances of dying just by speeding...

EIGHT

"I'm sure this house featured on a serial killer television special." Harry flapped his wings, lifted off Holly's moped, and settled onto her shoulder. "I counsel against entry, if you want to live."

Holly rolled her eyes at her raven's dramatics. "It's a little cottage garden that's a tad overgrown. The peeling paint on the building adds to the whole unloved serial killer impression. "We aren't here to buy real estate. We came for Arnold Twigg."

"Your life, but I reserve the right to tell you I told you so when someone wielding a hatchet jumps out at you." Harry sniffed and hopped off Holly's shoulder. He settled on the fence that bordered Twigg's property.

"It's secluded here. Lots of large trees, plenty of

space. Nice." Nate pushed a large, dark curl away from his face and prowled around the front yard. "This could be a peaceful place to settle, if it wasn't so unkempt."

"That's probably because Arnold's mother, Mabel, is living at the Eternal Rest Retirement Home. I bet she probably kept nagging Arnold to do the jobs, but he lapsed since she left."

"Responsibility for the aged isn't easy." Nate frowned, a disapproving expression upon his face. "Someone should have looked after her previous residence. People care about these things." He looked around. "It's very quiet."

"Elspeth used to have her witchshine stills out here because it was so quiet, but the neighbors didn't appreciate the wicked witch of Point Muse operating so close to them. They staged a protest and raided her stills. Eventually, she moved her operation. Plus, she's given up on her hipflask and the witchshine... *Mainly,*" Holly amended. "Everyone in town started carrying a hipflask and imitating her. She wasn't impressed with that. Elspeth prefers to be one-of-a-kind."

"That's because no one likes the Harrows. A pernicious breed of witches everyone prefers to avoid."

The low, gruff voice filtered from behind the rickety fence Harry sat on. An elderly man with wild, snowy white hair that stuck straight up popped his head over the fence. He glared at Holly. "You'd better not steal anything of Mabel's. I'm watching you, Harrow."

Squeaking, Harry stiffened and tipped off the fence, hitting the ground as taxidermy.

Nate took a step forward, placing himself in front of Holly, hands loosely at his sides. "We didn't come here to steal."

The old man cleared his throat and spat on the ground. "She's a Harrow, and I don't know you. Probably steal the house blind and then curse me."

Holly pushed out from behind Nate. "Why does everyone think we'll curse them?"

"Because your grandmother's evil." The old man whipped out a spray bottle with purple colored liquid and sprayed it directly into Holly's face. "Begone, Harrow demon."

Holly covered her face and moaned gutturally.

Grabbing Holly by the back of the shirt, Nate yanked her out of the way. The banshee hunched over, but he stood in front protecting her. The elderly man's bellow of laughter coincided with Holly's giggles.

"What in Hades is going on?" Nate roared at the gigglers.

Her laughter trailing off, Holly gasped in a few breaths and rubbed her aching ribs. "My protector." She fluttered her eyes and then shoved a still taxidermy Harry with her foot. "You, on the other hand, are a big Viking scaredy-cat...raven. Whatever." Holly beamed at the still snorting man on the other side of the fence. "How's it going, Able?"

The elderly man drew in a shuddering breath and sobered. "One of these days, I'll have a heart attack over our antics."

"You'll only have yourself to blame if it does happen. I'll make sure you're my priority burial of the day."

"Reassuring." Straightening, the older man held his hand over the fence. "Able Littleton."

Eyebrows beetled over his hazel eyes, Nate gingerly shook Able's hand. "I take it you two know each other."

Able winked. "I've known this little banshee since she was knee-high to a miniature racing unicorn."

"He pretends he's vanquishing evil Harrows with lavender spray." Holly shrugged. "It's our thing."

"Great. Next time warn a guy." Nate glared at the duo. "I thought you were being attacked."

"It's a highlight of an old man's life when the banshee visits." He cocked his head. "Why *are* you here? It's not visiting day."

"We're after Arnold Twigg. We have a few questions. Have you seen him today?"

"A little while ago, he came rushing back. My game show was on television, so I didn't pay much attention. What's that lazy excuse done now?"

"We just need to ask a few questions about people he's been seen with. How he makes his money."

Able snorted at Holly's words. "He pretends to work and sticks his nose into other people's business until they pay him to back off. That's how he makes money."

"Blackmail." Nate growled the word. "I don't remember much, but I know I hate blackmailers."

"Yeah. Poor Mabel. Wastrel for a son. He put her in the retirement home a while ago. The house just went downhill from there. She'd be horrified if she saw it now." Able shook his graying head sadly, faded blue eyes dim.

"If Arnold is a blackmailer, what does he spend his cash on?" Holly looked around the overgrown, unloved front yard. "Because it definitely isn't on the upkeep of his mom's house."

Opening his mouth to speak, Able shot Nate a guarded glance.

Holly waved at the older man. "That's Nate. He's fine. The Harrows are helping him find his missing marbles. What were you going to say?"

"I've seen him coming and going with boxes from electrical stores and such. When he's not working, he's always wearing brand-new duds."

"Have you seen anyone visiting recently?" Nate interjected with his own question.

"Bookies normally. He likes the racing 'corns. He's a gambler mostly. I did see someone the other day though, dressed up in a suit with a weird hat. Bookies aren't such snappy dresses normally. But I haven't seen the guy since."

"Thanks, Able."

"You two hang on a second." Able shuffled back inside his tidy cottage.

"Twigg's a gambler and had a guy in a suit visit him lately. Not much to go on." Nate rubbed the back of his neck. "But I guess we haven't searched the house yet."

Harry rolled to his feet and flapped his wings a few times. "By the state of the outside, I refuse to step one wing inside that cesspool. I shall guard your silver conveyance."

"In other words, you'll hide near Holly's moped. What a brave Viking." Nate mocked the bird and ducked as Harry lifted into the air, nearly colliding with his head.

"When you contract some virulent plague, I will crow I told you so." Harry zoomed toward the house and settled on the gutter.

"Able mentioned a suited man." Holly nibbled the edge of her lip. Suited men didn't exactly abound in Point Muse, although there were a few. Her great uncle Edgar, for one, loved to wear the odd suit. Although his were a tad threadbare. But Able mentioned a weird hat as well. And that fit just one person she was acquainted with. *Samuel Wood.*

"Here you go. I figure you'd want to take a look inside. Might as well not break and enter if you don't have to." Able threw a set of keys over the fence.

Snatching them out of the air, Nate nodded their thanks.

"Hey, Able? Did anything else stand out about the suited guy who visited Arnold?" Holly asked.

Thinking for a moment, Able nodded. "Just a weird looking hat. Old-fashioned, Like Grandad used to wear."

Nodding her thanks, Holly turned, heading for Twigg's cottage.

Nate joined the banshee on a porch crowded with empty boxes. "You thought of something?"

Twitching her nose, Holly rapped on the cottage door. "Let's just say the only suited guy I know who has a habit of wearing old-fashioned hats is Samuel Wood. Funny how his name keeps popping up."

When no one answered the door, Nate unlocked it and took a careful step into the front hallway. "You think your funeral director was blackmailed by Arnold?"

"I'm starting to think he might've been. Which leads me into wondering what he did in the first place to warrant paying someone to shut up." Stepping around a pile of half empty boxes, Holly shuddered. "Harry wasn't wrong about this place." She reached into an open box and drew out a fluffy, gray toy Chihuahua. "Not something I'd expected a janitor in his forties to hoard."

Nate rifled through another box and hefted out a hot pink hand weight. "I don't think this is Mr. Twigg's color either."

Snorting, Holly wandered into the box-filled sitting room.

"Either Arnold's a hoarder, or he's buying and

selling crap at a grossly inflated rate. He probably has shares in the shopping network."

Grimacing, Nate stepped over a small pile of plastic wrapped, glow-in-the-dark panties. "To be honest, it's near impossible to search for clues in this mess. I bet the whole house looks like this."

"I'm a Harrow. I don't take sucker bets. Let's check out the kitchen." Holly eased the door open and took one step inside before gagging. She slapped a hand over her mouth and scrambled for the partially open door that led outside.

"Holly, are you okay?" Nate hollered from behind her.

Bent over, Holly dragged deep breaths in and out. Her short, brown bob hung over her face as she fought to keep her breakfast down. "I'm fine. But I think I'll check the shed out here. The kitchen's nasty." Harry was right. Possible infection chances had increased tenfold after she stepped into the kitchen. Arnold needed housekeeping lessons, or he at least needed to throw out food instead of piling plate upon dirty plate on the counter. Holly felt her glands, relaxing when no lumps appeared.

Strolling toward the lopsided shed, Holly lifted her face to the sun streaming down. Soaking up the warmth, she gathered her composure and flung the door to the shed wide. Darkness stared back at her. "Why are sheds always so dark and gloomy?" A whoosh sounded from behind Holly, along with a gust of wind blowing on the back of her neck. With a shriek, Holly jumped forward and stepped on something sharp that crunched underfoot. Dancing around in the darkened shed, Holly's feet slid out from underneath her, and she fell heavily to the ground. Something soft broke her fall. "I hate sleuthing sometimes as much as I hate searching scary, dark sheds." She braced a hand against her soft landing. A small, black, feathered shape flew at the one window in the shed, clawing at the material covering the glass.

Light blasted the shed's interior, illuminating Harry at the window.

"You feathered-covered Viking. You scared the banshee out of me... *Almost.*"

Speaking of her banshee... Itching spread up Holly's arms, along with an almost painful pricking of her nerve endings. A bloodcurdling scream burst out of her, building and building, until Harry flew at her, producing a cool breeze that buffeted her face. Holly's scream dwindled and her banshee receded. She drew in shuddering breaths. Her banshee had absented itself from her for so long she'd forgotten what it felt like to have her gifts active. Lately her powers had been in the off position.

"Holly?" Harry hopped up onto the scarred wooden bench. "You might want to move your hand."

Looking down at her hand, clenched in the bloody shirt-wearing, obviously dead, Arnold Twigg, she let out another screech, this one more hysterical than mystical.

Nate burst through the open door, grabbed Holly in his arms, and carried her out of the shed, cradling her against his muscled chest. "What happened? Are you okay?"

"Arnold Twigg, dead in the shed. A broom handle through his chest." Holly had her head on Nate's chest, eyes closed tight. She might be a banshee who had death visions and worked in a funeral home, but discovering murder victims wasn't something she wanted to get used to.

"Is he really dead? Did you check for a pulse?"

Nate's voice rumbled under Holly's cheek. "Trust me. Broomstick through the chest. He's dead."

"Oh, he's definitely dead. Violent deaths are my thing, sweetie."

A shrill voice from the past shocked Holly into opening her eyes. An immaculate blonde woman in a power pink suit with boxy shoulder pads and long black talons met her shocked gaze. "Marie Hestis?"

"In the flesh...so to speak, darling." Marie beamed; her sharpened teeth gleaming. "And I'm here to collect a soul... So pay up."

NINE

"We spend so much time here, maybe we should bring our own furniture." Holly shifted on the metal chair. "A padded one."

"Do I want to know why you spend a lot of time in police stations?" Nate cocked his head, a dark curl falling over his forehead.

Holly fought the urge to push the wayward strand away. She sat on her hands just in case they decided to wander.

"We're Harrows. Comes with the territory."

Zach Braun, police chief, bear shifter, and now cousin by marriage, strode straight into the room and collapsed into a chair. "Give it to me."

Nate frowned. "Give you what, Chief?"

"The story, the dead guy. Whatever complicated

plan you've concocted. The usual Harrow shenanigans."

"This isn't my doing." Holly pointed at Nate. "It's all his fault. I found him chained in a coffin, with no memory. We've been trying to track his identity down, then people who died non-violent deaths started coming back alive. Arnold Twigg's been hanging outside the funeral home, and we saw him arguing with a nurse at the hospital. He seems shifty. We decided to search his office and then his house because we're pretty sure he's been blackmailing people. Then I found his body in the shed, and that crazed Marie Hestis turned up wanting souls." Holly took a breath and blew it out. "Phew. I feel much better now. It's unhealthy to keep things in." She beamed at the room.

"Right, then." Zach turned to Nate. "Anything to add? Any recovered memories yet?"

"Not really. Just vague impressions, nothing concrete. I know my name's Nate Mortis. But that's it."

"I'll run a search of the name and see what I turn up." Zach made another note in this file.

Holly leaned forward and rescued her trapped hands, then tapped the table. "What I want to know is why has Marie Hestis turned up again? I thought after she'd killed that daimon hag, she was supposed to take her place and leave us alone?"

Nate leaned forward, and a spark of interest transformed his face. "Daimon? Like a Keres daimon? The hags that collect souls that have had a violent demise?"

"Seems like you do remember some things." Zach narrowed his gaze on the suddenly twitchy Nate.

"Just flashes. That's all. When Holly mentioned daimons, I just had a flash of information."

"We've had a run-in with the Keres sisters before, when they escaped Hades. One of them was killed and the murderer was supposed to take her place." Holly glared at Zach. "Why is she here?"

Zach gathered his paperwork. "Twigg was murdered. Ms. Hestis is collecting his soul."

Holly pointed at Nate. "Violent death like he said."

"Correct. Point Muse law enforcement has been tasked with cooperating. And that's exactly what we're doing." Zach grabbed his papers and stood. "Not that you'll take my advice but maybe you should leave investigating Nate's incident to the police."

Holly opened her mouth to laugh loudly at the

chief's insinuation, but Elspeth burst into the interview room with a panting Colin at her feet.

Zach dropped his file on the table. "Okay, let's have it. It's best to ride this mayhem and let it play out."

"You'll never take them alive, copper." Elspeth threw an emerald-green ball on the floor and immediately dropped to her stomach, commando crawling to Holly.

Everyone stared at Elspeth and her electric blue wig with Shirley Temple style, corkscrew curls and matching velour jogging suit.

"Why are you crawling on the ground?" Her grandmother lived in the crazy, but this was over the top, even for the wicked witch of Point Muse.

"Shush. I'm down here. You can't see me, but I'm at your feet." Elspeth kept her eyes shut tight and tugged on Holly's jeans. "It's because of the smoke, that's why you can't see me. I'm here to break you out."

A scent of rotten egg and pungent damp mold settled into the room. Holly clapped a hand over her nose. She hunched her shoulders as a violent heave shook her skinny frame. "That wasn't a smoke bomb."

Zach covered his nose with his arm and mumbled into it.

"What?" Nate shook his head. "We can't hear you." He swallowed and valiantly tried to breathe as normal.

Shuddering, Zach moved his arm. "Why is it always the hard way with you Harrows?" The police chief tracked Elspeth as she writhed on the floor, like a directionless snake.

"The copper's distracted by the smoke. He doesn't know I'm here. So, stop, drop, and roll out of here, banshee," Elspeth hissed at her granddaughter. She wiggled until she faced the door. "Follow my lead." The wicked witch commando crawled forward and banged into Nate's leg. "Oops. Sorry, Amnesia Boy. But this is a covert breakout. Follow me."

"We. Can. See. You," Holly screeched and then blanched as she accidentally breathed in. "You used a stink bomb, not a smoke bomb. We can all see you rolling on the ground like a velour-covered caterpillar." She dry-retched and clapped a hand over her mouth. No one needed to see her tongue hanging out of her mouth.

"Oh." Elspeth cracked one eye open and then the other. "Why didn't you say something?"

Colin rolled his eyes, turned around, and trotted back out the door. "I think it's time for a snack break now that we've broken the banshee out of the big house."

"Argh." Dealing with her grandmother gave her a migraine or possibly one of Harry's tumors. Maybe banging her head repeatedly against a hard object would help.

Elspeth used Nate's jeans-covered legs to haul herself up. She flapped a hand in front of her nose. "You really let your housekeeping skills go since getting married. This room stinks."

"Out," Zach bellowed.

"Geez. Take a chill pill or a shower, copper." Elspeth smirked and strolled out. She paused in the open area filled with desks outside the interview room.

Aggie, Xandie's mother-in-law and police dispatcher, handed Holly some papers. "This is just a statement, sweetie. Sign, and Elspeth can escape without causing any more chaos." She winked at the wicked witch.

"What chaos?" Elspeth huffed. "I just rescued my granddaughter from the po po. It's always the quiet ones you have to watch...like Amnesia Boy." Elspeth narrowed her gaze on Nate. "That's if you still have memory problems?"

Holly rolled her eyes. "Yes, Elspeth. He still has amnesia."

"Okay, then." Elspeth's eyes tracked Nate as he shuffled on the spot.

"I think this is yours." Aggie held out a still taxidermy Harry. "He screeched at us that he had Viking rights and refused to squeal, then he taxidermied himself."

"So loyal." Holly tucked the bird under her arm and shot a glance over her shoulder at Nate. "Ready to go?"

"Not like he has any worldly gifts to tow behind him." Elspeth snorted and scratched at an arm. "I'm done. Law enforcement gives me hives." She stomped to the door and sped outside.

Following her grandmother's lead, Holly stepped outside and breathed slowly in and out, checking her pulse. Everything seemed fine. No sudden onset of illness caused by finding a body or by a short stay in a stinky police station. Holly called that a win-win situation.

"For all that is pure and good in Point Muse, loose me from your underarm or I will perish. I keep getting stuck under Harrow armpits. It isn't sanitary."

Harry's muffled voice drifted out from underneath Holly's arm, and she drew the mouthy bird out. "You're taxidermy. You can't perish or even be smothered."

"He can whine though." Nate shot the bird an amused smile. "Which he does, most of the time."

"At least he knows who he is. Most of the time." Elspeth tapped a foot, her blue corkscrew curls bouncing. "Same can't be said for you... *Can it?* Any memories yet? What about now? And now?"

"Leave him alone. He'll remember at his own pace." Holly brightened. "He did remember about the Keres daimons, so that has to be a good sign."

"Isn't that good timing?" Elspeth focused on Main Street. "I wonder if Lila has any brownies left. I have a powerful hunger now that I've rescued your jail-bound patootie."

"Exactly what I was thinking, my queen." Colin shook his pudgy pug body and jerked to attention. "I am ready for a snack mission anytime you are."

Elspeth's minion was always ready for food, any kind of food. The dog couldn't move two steps without claiming hunger. But come to think of it, a brownie or two wouldn't go astray. Holly rubbed her complaining stomach.

"The police were only questioning us, not detaining us." Nate ducked as Harry lifted into the air and hovered over the man's head for a moment, rifling through his curly dark hair with his sharp talons.

"Potato, potahto and all that jazz."

Holly tuned out their squabbling as she strode ahead, concentrating on the puzzle of Arnold Twigg and who had murdered the blackmailer. Samuel Wood, her fill-in funeral director, headed her list, but Leon and his suspicious nurse girlfriend were up there too. Nothing incriminating had popped up at Twigg's place, like shady photos, letters, or even a little blackmail book. Nothing to link anyone to Twigg but Holly knew there had to be something. She just needed to sleuth it out like Xandie did.

Two figures darted into a shadowy doorway ahead of them, drawing Holly's attention. A woman in her twenties poked her head out, peering along the street before disappearing again. Why would someone be watching them? The woman, with a short, black, pixie-cut hairdo, had looked strangely familiar. Where had Holly seen her before?

"Cat got your tongue, banshee? Has some contagious plague rotted your brains out of your head?" Elspeth stopped and faced her granddaughter, hands on hips. "Whatever beef you have, spit it out. I've got no time for lollygagging."

"I think someone's following us. *Maybe*," Holly amended.

"What? Where?" Nate spun, fists clenched. Hazel eyes flashing, he stepped in front of Holly, hands up and ready.

"Big, bad Amnesiac Boy to our rescue." Elspeth cackled. Shadows wriggled out and swam into every doorway before pooling at the wicked witch's feet like a rising blanket of mayhem and darkness. She clapped her hands and the light globe in the old-fashioned lamppost next to them shattered with a tinkle of glass. The shop window opposite them had a spider crack inching across the front window.

"Please stop hagging out. We can't afford to pay any more property damage." Holly massaged the back of her neck.

"I'm just flushing out any stalkers, banshee. Protecting the blood, so to speak."

"How about you protect my sanity and order me the biggest cappuccino Lila has?" Holly shoved Elspeth toward the bakery. "Go forth and annoy another of your grandchildren."

Elspeth curled her top lip. "I'm so underappreciated." The wicked witch slapped the bakery door open and stomped inside, muttering, as multiple customers crowded in with her.

Sighing, Holly waved Harry down. "Don't suppose you spotted any lurkers from the air?"

Harry ruffled his feathers and settled onto her shoulder. "Nope. I got nothing."

Even after Elspeth played the wicked witch and drained the shadows, they still hadn't spotted who'd been following them. Whoever had been watching must be strong to withstand Elspeth and keep their identity hidden. That's if they had been following them. Maybe Holly, Nate, and Elspeth hadn't been the stalking targets? Dropping the issue for now, Holly headed into the bakery and the extra-large, double dose of caffeine she deserved for dealing with Elspeth. Two women shouldered past Holly and paused in the doorway. The banshee moved out of the way, then stiffened as she recognized one of the customers. A woman with a short, black pixie haircut. The same one who had been watching them from a shadowy doorway. Faking normalcy, the banshee made a beeline for her usual table.

Nate followed, sidestepping around the two giggling women. One of the women, who had a long black braid, accidentally bumped into him and apologized.

Freezing for a moment, Nate nodded at the

women before following Holly to the Harrows' normal table.

The woman's companion opened and closed her mouth a few times, then ran a hand through her short hair. They stepped away from the door and put their heads together, whispering furiously as they stared at Nate.

"Looks like you have a fan club."

"I'm honored." He studiously ignored the whispering young women.

Nate's noncommittal answer raised Holly's hackles. "Methinks Amnesia Boy avoids the question."

Elspeth narrowed her own amber eyes on Nate. "Hiding things from a Harrow will be your downfall."

"What?" Nate looked up, surprised. "I'm not hiding anything. Just a bit of a headache."

"And the women?" Elspeth pressed.

"I just had a flash of pain and heard birds. Ravens cawing. That's all." Nate rubbed his forehead. "They seem familiar, but I could have seen them around town, for all I know."

"The ravens or the women?" Holly cocked an eyebrow.

"Could be a tumor." Harry flapped his wings from his perch on Holly's chair. "Pressing against your frontal lobe or pituitary and craniopharyngeal duct. You know, the normal spots."

"It's not a tumor," Nate ground out, flicking a glance at the two young women again.

"No more medical shows for you." Holly poked her raven in the stomach. The banshee jerked as a rough tongue bathed her ankle in canine saliva. "Ew. Dog eating my bare skin. Does anyone have wipes?"

"Sorry, sweet cheeks. But we both have a powerful hunger. Maybe you should feed us. Before we start looking at your skinny bones like chicken drumsticks." Colin stuck his head out from underneath the table and Nash, Lila's hellhound, followed suit.

"Dark man," Nash rumbled. His eyes flickered red before he rushed at Nate, leaping up. He placed his paws on the man's chest and shoved Nate's seat back a few paces as he proceeded to slather him in dog saliva.

"Whoa. Settle down, hound." Lila dumped a plate of decadent chocolate brownies in the middle of the table. "We don't bathe our customers; they can do it themselves. Eat this instead." Lila threw a muffin at Nash, who nabbed the baked good out of the air and offered half to Colin.

"Table service is a wonderful thing." The pug

snatched his share of the muffin from the hellhound and disappeared under the table.

Lila shook her head. "That hound's crazy about you, Nate. He's never like that. Not even with me." She regarded him suspiciously. "Did you bribe him?"

Nate held up his hands. "Nothing, I swear. Maybe it's just pheromones?"

"Yeah, you attract dogs." Elspeth opened her mouth to cackle, but Lila pointed a warning finger at her grandmother.

"Don't even hag out here. We're busy today, and I don't have time to deal with broken glass."

"Fine." Elspeth subsided. "Update us on the murder before the wicked witch gets bored."

Xandie jogged up to the Harrow table, panting. "Sorry I'm late. We had a rushed shipment of books on the chupacabra. What did I miss?"

"I want Holly to murder update us, but no one is talking and I'm getting bored."

Holly rushed into the sudden silence with an update. A bored Elspeth equaled Armageddon. "We found the janitor from the hospital, Arnold Twigg, dead in his shed. Broken broomstick through his chest. We think he was blackmailing people." Holly lowered her voice. "Maybe my fill-in boss from the funeral home. And we definitely saw him arguing with a nurse from the hospital. She's the girlfriend of the funeral home's gravedigger. And..." Holly opened her eyes wide. "Marie Hestis turned up at the murder, and Zach told us we need to cooperate with her. *Officially.*"

"What?" Lila and Xandie exclaimed together.

"I know. I'm like the proverbial bad penny and all that." Marie Hestis popped up at the Harrow table in her pink, shoulder-padded power suit. She spotted the platter of cakes. "Wahoo. Brownies. My down-fall." She reached out a hand.

"No brownies for people who try to kill me for my recipes." Lila yanked the plate away.

Marie pouted and picked her claws clean. "My new sisters warned me about prejudice from my past." Marie dropped her claw and beamed at the Harrows. "But I'm much happier as a daimon collecting souls who've died violent deaths than heading up a multinational company selling baked goods."

"Yay for you." Lila gathered her brownies to her chest and sniffed.

"I know. It's nice to have a new set of life goals. Speaking of life." Marie arched an eyebrow. "Seen any dead alive people hanging around?" She glanced around. "I've heard you have an epidemic."

Lila glared. "I'm going to call my dad. See what he thinks about people not dying and the daimon hag turning up. *And* I'm getting away from you, Ms. Hestis, and taking my brownies with me."

"Good idea. They're too much of a temptation." Marie glanced around at the busy bakery. "I figure that's why this place is so busy. Why otherwise would people come here?"

"Why you..." Lila bit her tongue, turned around, and stomped back into the kitchen.

Holly glared at the daimon. As she did so, she noticed the two young women from earlier sidling toward the bakery door, obviously eavesdropping on the conversation. "Just spit it out, Hestis. We don't have all day and there are prying ears around."

"You're no fun." The daimon sobered, all humor draining away. "There's been rumors in the underworld. *Death is missing.*"

Xandie shrugged. "Everyone's allowed a vacation."

"Not like this. Death normally arranges a fill in. This time, nothing. People dying are just getting up and walking around. It's upsetting the balance of life and death. And frankly, ticking off my new sisters. It makes them moody. Apparently, Thanatos is their half-brother. So, I'm here to assess Point Muse for culpability and act accordingly." Marie smirked. "The town has a reputation. The next few days should be awesome. Ciao, Harrows." Waving her newly minted daimon claws, Marie Hestis strolled out of the bakery.

"That's not good."

"That's an understatement, Xandie." Holly ground her teeth. Lila's former nemesis hanging over their heads like the sword of Damocles didn't bode well for a mayhem free week. The two whispering women caught the banshee's attention again as they shuffled out of the bakery in the opposite direction to the daimon hag. A snap decision to follow them grabbed hold of Holly. She stood and snapped fingers at Nate and Harry. "I think it's time we took a turn at stalking, boys."

Because those girls have suspicious written all over their sneaky, giggling, eavesdropping faces. Time for me to take a leaf out of Xandie's book and Sherlock up.

TEN

"Why are we here again?" Nate raised a hand and helped Holly climb over the fence at the back of the Mayweather Inn property. He held her tight for a few seconds once Holly was on stable ground. His rich hazel eyes met her amber ones.

Soda pop bubbles erupted in the pit of Holly's stomach, and she swallowed the lump that magically appeared in her throat. "What's the question again?" As she stared at Nate, the rushing noise of wings flapping had her subconsciously ducking. Mocking laughter filled her senses and the banshee slumped to the ground. Her vision silvered and her skin itched.

"You picked up a plague from the grave and have affected the banshee. The killer is likely your death.

Prepare yourself." Harry divebombed Nate, talons extended.

"I wasn't in the grave. Just the coffin. And all I did was help Holly over the fence." Nate hissed as Harry's talons connected with skin. "I don't want to hurt you, bird. It's Holly I'm concerned about."

Shaking her head, Holly pushed herself up from the ground and forced the banshee vision back, focusing on the raven versus man fight unfolding in front of her. "Oi. You two. Cut it out. It wasn't a plague. It was my banshee gifts flexing for once." Holly blinked her eyes a few times to clear the silver from her gaze. The last few months, her banshee gifts had been unreliable...*more unreliable than normal.* Even if she wouldn't admit it out loud, her gifts had never been that stable to begin with. Too much Harrow blood tended to cause chaos with the banshee side. But since Nate had entered her life, her inner banshee had decided to speak up. The question was why.

"What happened? One minute, we were talking, the next you were on the ground." Nate leaned worriedly in but stopped short of touching her skin. Instead, he smoothed her shiny, brown bob flat.

Gulping, Holly fought the urge to simper and flutter her eyelashes. Elspeth would be appalled.

"Banshee thing. I heard ravens and someone laughing."

Harry settled on the fence and glared at Nate. "I swear no ravens of my acquaintance would mock a banshee."

"Of course not. Perish the thought." Holly rubbed the back of Harry's neck. "Sorry I scared you."

"Hmmm." Harry leaned into Holly's stroking. "As long as the potential playboy keeps his hands to himself, you'll remain healthy."

"You sure you're okay? We don't need to follow those women if you need to rest." Nate shuffled his feet, glancing over his shoulder at the inn.

Someone suddenly looked more nervous than a simple stalking would normally engender. What was up with Nate?

"I'm good. Why don't you stick around outside? See if they come back out and I'll head inside. Speak to Rose." Holly eyed Harry and made a snap decision. She stared meaningfully at the Viking raven. "Why don't you stay with Nate? Make sure he's okay here." She lowered her eyelid in a subtle wink.

"No. I'm fine."

"Stay with playboy? Never."

Their words clashed as man and bird glared at each other.

Holly tapped Harry on the head. "Rose doesn't like you, Harry. She might talk more if you're not with me." Holly opened her eyes wide and darted them left and right. "Besides, this way, you can make sure no one bothers Nate. You can keep an eye on him, make sure he's safe." The banshee glared at her bird.

"I will not. I... I. Maybe that's a good idea." Finally getting it, Harry squawked and lifted off the fence into a nearby branch. "Hate for Amnesia Boy to be jumped by another Point Muse monster. I should be on guard." He bobbed his head up and down in agreement.

"I don't need a keeper," Nate ground out. He paced up and down on the back lawn. His curly hair flopped into his eyes, and with a muttered curse, he pushed it back. "I can be of use to you inside the inn. What happens if you have another banshee vision?"

"Since they mainly seem to be happening around you, I'm sure I'll be fine." Holly forced a smile. Nate seemed harmless, but between her visions and the way he wanted her to give up following the women from the bakery, she wasn't sure she could trust him one hundred percent. "Keep an eye out. And no fighting." Hoping they'd pay attention to her words but knowing they probably wouldn't, Holly double timed it to the back entrance of the inn.

Taking a deep breath, she settled her nerves and stepped inside the old Victorian house that had been turned into an inn and was now run by one of Aphrodite's descendant's, Rose Mayweather. Not a fan of the Harrow family, in fact, Rose detested the Harrows, but she was afraid enough of Elspeth that sometimes she'd let information slip. Holly was just used to Xandie or Lila taking the lead.

"Time to banshee up and get your big-girl sleuthing panties on." Holly strolled toward the reception desk. "Fake it until you make it."

"Why is it when anything goes wrong at Mayweather Inn, there's always a Harrow around? You're all harbingers of doom, including that mangy bird of yours." Rose craned her neck, trying to spot Harry. "Where did you leave it? He's hiding around the corner waiting to terrorize me, isn't he?"

Rose's silvery blonde, beehive style hairdo listed to one side, and she absently pushed it back to the center of her head as she glared at Holly. The lilac petticoats under her nineteen fifties style dress swished as she shuffled.

"Relax, Rose. I left Nate and Harry outside."

"Oh." The older woman blew out a breath. "That's good. I don't need any more issues right now."

Holly frowned and took a second look at the inn owner. Her silver hairdo might be piled up in the center of her head now, but it appeared scraggly, like she'd been dragged through a bush backward. And her dress was twisted to one side as if she'd tugged on it one too many times. Her cheeks blazed bright red. Holly moved back a few steps in case of contagion. "What's wrong? Are you getting sick?"

Rose threw her hands up in the air. "I swear, it seems like Mayweather Inn's jinxed." She narrowed her eyes at Holly. "Has Elspeth hexed my inn lately?"

"Not that I know of. Normally she'd lurk in the area to observe her handiwork, so if she isn't here, then it probably wasn't her."

Blowing out a breath, Rose hunched over her reception desk. "That's what I'm afraid of. I've had more customers check out in the last twenty-four hours than I have in six months. And I've only had two giggling girl's check in the other day. It's not likely I can make my money back anytime soon."

Two giggling girls sounded like the women from the bakery. "Did your customers start checking out around the time those girls checked in?"

"Around the same time, I guess."

Nice to be proved right. Elspeth always hates coincidences. "Any idea why the mass exodus from your inn?"

"Strife and discord. That's what it is." Rose struck points off her fingers. "Blockage in our pipes, intermittent hot water, lights and power flickering, squirrel infestation downstairs. Twenty-four hours of nothing but mayhem." She dropped her hands. "The milk soured this morning. The only customers eating tonight are those girls in the dining room. They just want fried food. Easy to prepare at least."

"I can ask Elspeth if she can help you out. You'll owe her but the inn will be back to normal."

Rose bit her lip, indecision spreading over her face. "I'll think about it. Now, shoo, Harrow. I've got squirrels to chase out of my bar."

"Have fun." Sounded like the chaos started when the girls from the bakery checked in. Maybe it was time to have a word with them. "You can do this, Holly Harrow. You have sleuthing in your bones." Girding herself, she pushed the door to the dining room open. Pausing for a moment, she spotted the young women sitting next to the windows that faced onto the front of the property. The inn's dining room featured heavily polished wood walls and furniture, but that was offset by the large bay windows that faced the inn's gardens.

Holly headed straight to the women who had their heads together, whispering and peering out the window. Holly checked the view and spotted Nate running from tree to tree near the fence line with his hands over his head. She sighed. "You just can't leave those two alone." It was pretty obvious that Harry had chased Nate around to the front of the building.

The young women with the short pixie cut and clearly defined, muscled arms snorted. "It's so funny. The Viking raven keeps dropping branches on the guy's head."

"Dinner and a show." The other woman, with a long black braid flipped over her shoulder, smirked. "Maybe we should pay the owner for the extra entertainment? She seems like she needs it. This place is pretty quiet. Although the bar seems to be hopping." She snickered and then covered it by taking a large mouthful of fried fish followed by a chaser of French fries.

How did the other girl know about Harry being a Viking? And why did she get the feeling they were both enjoying the strife and discord affecting the inn? "This place has had a few issues in the last twenty-four hours. Since right around the time you checked in." Holly beamed. "Isn't that a weird coincidence?"

Pixie-cut girl opened her dark brown eyes wide. "I know. Strange, isn't it? But then we heard Point Muse has all sorts of weird occurrences because of the ley lines."

Nodding, Braid Girl swallowed her bite of fried food. "That's why we're here. Our whole family loves weird. We're scouting out the town before our parents arrive in the next few days."

"Nice." Holly didn't believe a word of their explanation. "Why were you following my friend and me earlier, on Main Street?"

"What friend?" Pixie Girl fluttered her eyes.

Holly nodded at the show outside. "Bad boy out there."

"He's a friend? How close a friend?" Braid Girl leaned her chin on her hand, staring at Holly. "Must be nice to have such a good-looking friend. Or maybe it's more? He looks like he'd be a wonderful boyfriend for the right person."

The conversation had just detoured into uncomfortable.

"He's a friend like I said, and I still want to know why you two are following us."

"You must be imagining things. But it *is* Point

Muse. In fact, we heard a rumor a woman and a man had found a body earlier. Was that you and your *friend?*" Pixie Girl put emphasis on friend.

"And you're a banshee, right? Holly Harrow? If you did find the body, how come you didn't see it in a vision first?" the other woman chimed in, both women looking at Holly expectantly.

Point Muse was small, but rumor and gossip didn't normally move that swiftly. So, how did they find out that fast? "Yes, my name is Holly, but my banshee gifts aren't up for discussion with strangers."

"Then let's not be strangers." Pixie Girl trilled a high-pitched laugh. "I'm Ris and this is my sister, Patty."

"Not strangers now." Patty winked. "We heard it was that janitor guy who bought the farm. Murdered."

"You hear a lot." Way too much information for tourists to stumble across.

"We have friendly faces. And like we said, this town has a rep for murderous intentions." Patty stared thoughtfully at Holly. "Shadows hide all sorts of intentions. Even the most benign face can mask a killer."

That isn't creepy at all. Holly flashed back to the warm shadow she'd seen in her first vision when she'd touched Nate's chains. Shadows filled with birds cawing and fluttering, warmth all around. The banshee hadn't felt coldness or evil, but Patty had a point.

"We saw that janitor. Short and rotund, right?" Ris joined the conversation. "We saw him with some blonde nurse, arguing outside the bakery earlier. Then we spotted the woman getting into a car with some skinny, gray-haired guy who couldn't stop twitching. Maybe we should let your town cops know what we saw?"

Arnold Twigg, arguing with Callista, who then got into a car with Leon. What were the odds of that? Definitely time to speak to Callista and Leon. "You should help the local cops out. Tell them what you saw."

"Maybe. It's a thought." Ris winked at Holly.

The strident noise of a smoke alarm broke into the conversation, ringing through the empty dining room. The doors to the room swung open and Rose Mayweather stood highlighted in the doorway. "Everyone out. We have a small issue in the kitchen. Nothing serious, but you need to evacuate right now. Purely a safety measure." Rose glared until the girls stood.

The acrid odor of smoke and grease drifted into

the room. *That's it.* Holly was out. Death by grease fire wasn't the way she wanted to go. Without a backward glance, Holly headed into the foyer. The door to the bar was propped open and people filed out, including Sissy Corey, Mrs. Anti-Claus, who glowered at everyone as she stepped onto the porch. Out of the corner of her eye, Holly spotted the weird sisters freeze as they saw the patrons vacating the bar. The girls took a left turn and headed out the back. Who were they avoiding and why?

Holly joined the evacuation line and stepped onto the porch. She watched as Nate and Harry slipped around the side of the inn toward the back as well. Looked like Ris and Patty weren't the only ones avoiding people in the inn. Holly tabled the issue for later.

For now, Leon and his girlfriend were next on her agenda.

ELEVEN

"Why do I get the feeling you're experienced with breaking and entering?" Nate crowded in behind Holly, hiding her actions from prying eyes.

A shiver tracked down Holly's spine from the base of her neck. Nate wasn't touching her, so no chance of banshee visions, but his body warmth radiated out, heating her back. *Ignore...ignore...ignore,* Holly chanted in her mind. The last thing she needed was her family getting wind of her interest in Nate. Next thing, the Harrow spinster and Amnesia Boy would be set up on a blind date... *Hang on.* Holly froze. Since when did she have an interest in Nate? She was just making sure he wouldn't sue her or the funeral home for malpractice. *That's all.*

"Problems getting in?"

Nate's low voice tickled Holly's bare neck. "Nope. All good." She hurriedly shoved the door to Leon's apartment open and slipped Elspeth's purloined skeleton key finger into the pocket of her jeans. "And it's not breaking when you have a key, just entering."

"Somehow, I don't think your cousin's police chief husband would agree."

"What happens on a Harrow sleuthing mission stays on a Harrow sleuthing mission. Zip it." Holly stepped into the sparsely furnished apartment. "I'm glad I left Harry at home this morning. You two couldn't be quiet if your lives depended on it."

"He has an attitude problem." Nate slipped into the apartment and closed the door behind him. "And Harry only stayed at home because he hates early morning. Apparently, chasing me at the inn yesterday exhausted his taxidermy bones."

Holly flapped a piece of paper at Nate. "I didn't have a choice. Leon is working at the funeral home this morning, and I have a revised work schedule for him. It's important and our excuse to visit."

"If he's at the funeral home working, I'm pretty sure he knows about the schedule," Nate pointed out logically.

Holly rolled her eyes. "This morning, he got

called in by Samuel, nothing to do with normal schedule, and I'm not supposed to be working today. I'm pretending to helpfully drop this off. It's an excuse and I get bonus points for being proactive and dedicated to my job. Nah, nah." Holly poked her tongue at Nate.

Letting out a rich, deep, masculine chuckle, Nate patted Holly on the head. "Careful where you put that tongue, banshee. It might get you into trouble." He slid past and nosed around the small apartment. "Leon's not one for clutter, or comfort for that matter."

Holly banished the images of just where her tongue might disappear to and cleared her throat. "Leon's not a big socializer either. He doesn't join my team for after work drinks or coffee catch-ups. But he's only been here for a little while. Some people take more time to warm up than others. At least, that's what I thought up 'til now." Holly searched through the kitchen, but her gravedigger employee only had the bare minimum of utensils, plates, and other kitchen equipment in the cupboards.

"Maybe he keeps to himself for a reason?"

"Possibly. He does have a girlfriend though. Does that give him redeeming qualities?" Wandering into the bedroom, Holly trailed a finger over a bureau that faced a made-up double bed. "At least he cleans. It could be worse. Arnold Twigg worse." Holly shuddered at the memory of the dead janitor's hoarder's heaven.

Nate joined Holly in the bedroom. "I guess it depends on the girlfriend. Did he meet her here in town?"

Holly shook her head. "From what I gather, she followed him down here. I think we're going to need to speak to both Leon and Callista and ask them what their relationship is with the dead janitor."

"Is a sock with a rolled-up wad of cash inside it suspicious?" Nate stood next to an open drawer and held up a sock with a bulge in the heel area.

"Maybe he's saving for more furniture?" But a hidden pile of cash was definitely in the weird category.

Holly poked at Leon's bed, lifting one side of the mattress a few centimeters to peer under. "Nothing hidden under his mattress, but he has serious hospital corners going on."

"Maybe because he works in a hospital?"

"He mows lawns and digs graves. I'm pretty sure he's never made a bed in a hospital before but what about prison? I think they do hospital corners... Don't they?" *Now that's a thought.* Did Leon have a secret past? Had he done time? Was he running from something or someone? Holly moved to Leon's side table and rifled through the contents. A plain manila envelope caught her attention. Reaching inside, Holly drew out promotional flyers and pamphlets, all advertising Point Muse. "I guess he wanted to be prepared when he moved." She held up a flyer touting the benefits of living in Point Muse.

Nate replaced the money sock back in the drawer and strolled over to Holly, peering at the different flyers. "It's like an information packet someone would be supplied with if they were in witness protection."

"Or a spy. Or a travel agent's packet of background information on a vacation destination. That type of thing." Holly looked up at Nate to find him staring down at her. His scent wrapped around her, cocooning her in a masculine warmth that caused her pulse to trip. Holly dropped her gaze and shoved the flyers back into the folder. "I don't think we'll find anything else here. And we need to get out before we get caught." She slid the folder into the drawer, making sure to put it back in the same spot.

Stepping away, Nate exhaled and nodded. "What's our next step?"

"Speak to some of his neighbors? And his girl-friend, Callista."

Nate bowed gracefully. "After you, banshee."

"Thanks, Amnesia Guy." Holly snorted at her lame reply. She made a determined effort to push his musky, woody scent out of her mind as she relocked the apartment behind them. "Let's head down to the mailboxes and pretend we're looking for Leon, to give him his new work schedule."

"Lead on, fearless leader." Nate winked.

Argh. The charm offensive was gnawing away at her control. Holly stopped at a wall of mailboxes and an older woman, who stood shuffling through her mail. "Hi. Excuse me?" Holly smiled sweetly at the lady.

"What can I do for you?" The woman finished looking at her mail and turned her attention to the strangers. "You aren't debt collectors, are you?" She eyed Nate's muscled arms and slim waist. "Although, come to think of it, I might have cash in my apartment." She winked.

Nate stepped behind Holly. "I'm just here to support her." He nudged the banshee forward.

Rolling her eyes, the banshee took the lead. She waved the revised timetable. "I work with Leon, and I have a new schedule for him, but he's hard to track down. I've tried his apartment already. I was wondering if you have any idea where he might be?"

"Leon." The woman grimaced. "Sorry if he's a friend of yours."

Holly snorted. "Nope. I just work with him."

"Phew." The woman smirked. "My mouth tends to engage before my brain. Leon's kind of a hermit. He works at the funeral home and the hospital far as I know."

"I'm from the funeral home. But I'm not at work today. I thought I'd just drop this off while I was shopping in town."

"If he isn't at work, he might be at his girlfriend Callista's place. She has a little place on the edge of town. You can't miss it. It's that fake, pink ginger-bread cottage." The woman grimaced. "Looks girly and sweet, but its occupant isn't. She gives you the impression of a high school mean girl. Thankfully, they both keep to themselves."

Holly frowned. "Does he have any friends he hangs with? They might be able to pass on the schedule."

"Not in this apartment building. I have heard him talking to some guy with a posh accent and weird taste in clothing. Old-fashioned with a top hat kind of thing." The woman stared off into the distance for a moment before focusing back on Holly. "I did see him let someone into the apartment the other night. It was really weird. The person wore a big, hooded, black cloak. The kind you see in a fantasy movie or a fairytale. Old but fancy. I didn't see the face, and they wore matching gloves. Saw it when the person knocked. I guess that's not much help." She shrugged.

"More help than you think." Top hat? Old-fashioned clothing and a snooty accent? Sounded like Samuel *"Woo-Woo"* Wood, the fill-in funeral director. But why would he bother talking to a gravedigger at home? Normally, he'd tell Holly to do it. Why come all the way out to Leon's apartment? More and more questions. "Maybe I'll just put it in his mailbox. Thanks for your help." Holly forced a smile and shoved the schedule into Leon's mail slot.

"No worries." The woman looked Nate up and down. "If you get bored being moral support, I'm next door to Leon." She waggled her fingers at Nate and headed back into her apartment.

He blew out a breath and moved back from Holly. "I've never felt more like a piece of meat before. She looked like she was cataloguing my every flaw."

Holly patted Nate's scruff-covered face. The

stubble pricked her skin, and she snatched the hand away, rubbing it along her patchy jeans leg. "I don't think it was your flaws she was cataloguing. More like checking your body out."

"I prefer not to think about it." Nate changed the subject. "I take it we're heading to search the nurse's house now?"

"Nope. Not yet. I want to check in at Harrow House first. Pick up Harry. I'm pretty sure I know who Leon's been talking to."

Samuel seemed to be way more involved in Point Muse shenanigans than a temporary funeral director should be. Holly needed to find out why.

"I thought Elspeth never let anyone into her evil lair?" Nate pointed to the open door of the shed and the police cruiser parked in front.

Holly slid off her moped and dropped her helmet into the bird carry basket attached to the front. "Suddenly, I have this feeling I should get back on my moped and skedaddle out of here."

"Too late," Nate intoned as Elspeth appeared in the doorway of the shed.

"You fiend," the wicked witch shrieked. "I told

you to stay out of my cave. You'll rue the day you didn't listen. I have a nasty payback with your name engraved all over it."

"Hey. Timeout." Holly stepped up next to Nate and faced her grandmother. "He's been with me. And we've been searching Leon's apartment and speaking to his neighbors. No one has been in your shed. You're barking up the wrong amnesiac."

"Amnesiac. Ha." Elspeth barked a laugh. "He knows more than he lets on, and he has broken into my cave before."

"Egged on by the bird. He told me it was fine to look." Nate shook his head. "I've stayed out since then. Whatever's happened, it wasn't me." He held up his hands.

Zach Braun, Holly's cousin's husband, appeared next to the wicked witch. "He isn't lying. Melody just radioed in that she saw Holly and Nate heading into Point Muse apartments. It wasn't him."

Huffing, Elspeth crossed her arms over her hot pink velour jogging suit. "Then who else would steal my chain?"

"What?" Holly squeaked. "Someone stole the chain?"

"The same chain I was wrapped in at the funeral home? That you were taking care of?" Nate rubbed the back of his neck. "That's not good. I don't want to end up with chains again."

"Someone broke in and stole the chain. Did they take anything else?" Holly stepped up to Elspeth and poked her head around her grandmother, peering into the cave.

"You aren't welcome either, banshee. I only let the fuzz in so he could get crime scene evidence. Yank your nose out of my business." Elspeth stepped in front of Holly, blocking her view.

"The only thing left behind was this tiny bit." The police chief held up a small link of chain.

"I thought the chain had been crafted by Hephaestus, the Greek god. How did the link break off?" Nate furrowed his brow and looked confused.

Elspeth smirked and blew on her bright colored nails which matched her bubblegum-pink, curly, shoulder-length wig. "I got skills. I've been analyzing it. Why don't you let the banshee hold it? She might get a vision of who violated my lair."

Zach held out the chain to Holly who gingerly took it in hand.

"Whoever stole the rest of the chain probably wore gloves. I won't get anything." An itch started in the palm of the hand that held the chain. It spread like ants marching along her arm. Fog bled into the corners of her sight, obscuring Elspeth. Holly's head snapped back as a scream spilled out of her mouth, an undulating wail that grew in volume. An image scrolled past her silver eyes of a car, speeding, unable to stop. Then an image of the cemetery. Open graves. The picture dissipated to be replaced by a hooded figure in an ornate black velvet cloak followed by the overwhelming feeling of cold, unforgiving death.

"Breathe, Holly. Just breathe."

A warm hand on her arm broke the banshee vision with a snap. Holly drew a ragged breath before focusing on Nate's hand. She lifted her head and stared into rich hazel eyes. "Thanks. Sometimes my inner banshee takes charge and won't let go. I'm still learning how to deal with her and the visions."

"Happy to help." Nate let his hand drop away.

Holly immediately felt cold again. She held out the chain to Elspeth. "I think you can hold onto this now."

Elspeth took the chain and slipped it into the pocket of her jogging suit. "What did you see?" For once, a serious expression graced the witch's face.

"A figure wearing a cape. A car speeding, and an open grave at the funeral home. An overwhelming feeling of cold death." Holly shrugged. "That's all. No faces or anything recognizable."

"I can't put an all-points-bulletin out on a caped figure." Zach rubbed his forehead. "I need to head back to the station. Let me know if you see anything actionable." He pointed at Elspeth. "And you calm down and stop accusing innocent bystanders of crimes. It gives me indigestion." He waved at Holly and headed back to his cruiser.

"You'll still never take me alive, copper," Elspeth bellowed and stepped back into her lair, slamming the door shut with a bang.

"Welcome to the crazy that is the Harrow family." Holly offered a weak smile. "At least you don't have a mouthy, cursed Viking raven dive bombing you."

"Just the wicked witch and a pretty little banshee." Nate winked. "I think I can deal with that kind of crazy."

If only it were that easy...

TWELVE

"It's your day off. So, why do I see you and your so-called family member here?"

Samuel Wood stood in front of Holly, resplendent in a heavy brown frock coat that ended just above his knees, with matching trousers and a dove gray waistcoat he'd paired with a crisp white shirt. His faded blue eyes blinked rapidly until he narrowed his gaze on Holly. "Do you have an answer for me, Ms. Harrow?"

His plummy accent scratched at Holly's last nerve. In fact, you could say it was a snooty accent. Samuel was definitely the man Leon had been seen arguing with. The question was, why would the snooty funeral director associate with a gravedigger? Unless Samuel had an ulterior motive? Holly smiled at the funeral director. "Why, Samuel, I just love my job. I can't get enough of the funeral home, and I decided to give my cousin, Nate, a tour. For some reason, he loves funeral homes." The banshee beamed.

Samuel's eyes flickered to Nate's form lurking behind Holly. "The funeral home is not a tourist attraction, Ms. Harrow. I think you should leave and return when you're scheduled for work."

"Really? I think more people touring the funeral home, making sure everyone's practices are above-board so potentially damaging accidents don't occur, would be a smart idea." Nate crossed his arms over his chest, biceps flexing under his plain T-shirt.

Holly's mouth filled with spit, and she swallowed a few times, so she didn't spray people when she spoke. "He has a point, don't you think? I'd hate for any serious accidents to occur, like unscheduled burials." Holly dumped her words into a momentary lull in the conversation.

Samuel stiffened and his eyes flickered over the banshee's shoulder to Nate. He wiped a bead of sweat off the side of his face. "Fine. But you are not here to work. Understand me?" The funeral director spun to stomp away but paused and turned back. "Where is that cursed familiar of yours?"

Holly airily waved a hand. "He's hanging around somewhere. He's a curious Viking and does what he wants."

"*Hmph.* Some of us need to get back to work." Samuel muttered unintelligible words under his breath as he marched off.

"Charming man."

"Who has a snooty accent and likes to wear weird, old-fashioned, Victorian style clothing and sometimes a top hat. Remind you of anyone?" Samuel just kept popping up with Leon or the late Arnold Twigg. Whatever was going on, the funeral director was in the thick of it.

Nate picked up the reference immediately. "He's the man the neighbor saw arguing with Leon."

"And he's been seen at the hospital talking to the dead janitor too. I think Mr. Wood has some questions to answer." Holly grabbed Nate's hand and towed him down the hallway. "We need to find Leon. Let's ask Dolly at the front desk."

"Dolly?"

"She's the receptionist. She's also the younger sister of two of my team. Doug and Dave."

Holly slid to a stop in front of a large, ornate stone desk. "Hey, Dolly. Have you seen Leon anywhere this morning? I need to have a chat with him."

"Holly. Thank goodness you're here." The troll receptionist slid a phone farther under her cheek as she asked the caller to hold. Placing a hand over the mouthpiece, she waved a file at the banshee. "Can you take this to Samuel, please? Apparently, he needs it urgently." She rolled her moss-green eyes. "As for Leon, I think I saw Harry follow him outside."

"Thanks, Dolly." Holly grabbed the file detailing the funeral home's financials and raised an eyebrow. Samuel was way too interested in the inner workings of her workplace for her liking. The sooner her absent bosses returned the better. She waved the file and headed back toward Samuel's temporary office.

"What's important about that file?" Nate kept pace with Holly.

"Financials on the funeral home. One wonders why a temporary employee wants to know specifics like that." Holly grinned maliciously, then let out a cackle reminiscent of her grandmother. "And I think I'll ask him just that." The closer they drew to Samuel's office, the louder his muffled voice became. "Sounds like good old Samuel is having a tiff on the phone."

Holly grabbed Nate's arm and dragged him into a sitting room next door to the funeral director's office. She lifted a small oil painting of flowers off the wall. "No one trusts Samuel. The last time he filled in, he kept disappearing into his office for hours on end. We found out this wall has some unique features." She placed her ear against the wall and squinted as she listened.

"In other words, the walls are thin, and you can eavesdrop."

Holly winked but focused on Samuel's muffled words.

"Everything is fine. I have complete control of the situation."

Samuel's words trickled in but made no sense to Holly... Yet.

"That wasn't my fault. Do you understand? Not my fault." Samuel bit out the words and slammed the phone down with a curse.

Grabbing the painting, Holly slipped it back into place.

"He's in control and it's not his fault." Nate raised an eyebrow. "Do you think he's talking about me or you?"

"I think it's time I deliver the paperwork. You

hang back. He might be more talkative if you're not looming."

"Good luck with that. He doesn't strike me as the most talkative or approachable man."

"You have no idea." Holly gripped the file tight and made a beeline for Samuel's office. She paused and listened for a moment before banging on the door.

"What?" Samuel roared.

Holly cracked the door open and waggled the file. "Sorry to interrupt your day, but Dolly was busy on the phone and wanted me to drop this off."

"Fine." Samuel waved Holly forward.

She slapped the file on the desk. "Interesting reading. Why do the funeral home's financials matter when you're only here for a while?"

"I like to be informed across all aspects of the funeral business when I take a position. And my interest's not only in death rituals of supernatural creatures but accounting as well. Not that it's your business." Samuel glared.

Interesting combination. She'd worked with the man a few times now and knew he was a warlock of middling power, specializing in death rituals. But Holly had never heard about his love of accounting before. "Speaking of the funeral business, have you heard from Hector and Hillary lately?" Holly perched on the edge of the desk and absentmindedly checked her pulse as she waited for him to reply.

"Your employers are tied up with their family business and will give us notice of their return date when they have one." Samuel grabbed a pencil and jabbed at Holly. "Desks are not for sitting on. The lax actions of the employees of this funeral home are concerning." He dropped the pencil and stood, pushing his chair behind him before he walked to the door. "In fact, it would benefit everyone, and you in particular, to review your business practices. Who knows?" He shrugged. "My position may very well become permanent, and if it does, there will be sweeping changes. Now, if you will excuse me, one of us needs to do some work." He gestured to the door.

"That's fine." Holly drew level with Samuel. "I need to speak to Leon, anyway. Remember Leon? Our gravedigger? Such a lovely man. He has a way with words." She raised an eyebrow at Samuel whose face paled. "See you later, Samuel." Holly slipped past the funeral director, making sure to brush her hand over his as she did. Maybe she could get a banshee vision that would answer a question.

Samuel slammed the door shut behind the banshee, leaving her and Nate alone in the hallway.

A cold chill wrapped around Holly, squeezing tight, choking the air from her lungs. She struggled to breathe until warm bands wrapped around her, dissipating the malevolent, bitter wind that had tried to choke her. Holly snuggled into the nearest source of heat and let the warmth flush the chill away.

"You okay, now?"

Cracking one eye open, Holly realized she'd snuggled against Nate like a leech sucking his life force. Squeaking, she pushed against the defined muscles of his chest. "Sorry. Sometimes I'm a heat-seeking parasite when I come down off a banshee vision." Nate's resulting laugh rumbled under Holly's hands, and she dropped them away quickly. "You can let me go now. I'm okay."

"You sure? You looked like you were struggling to breathe. "

"When I touched Samuel, it felt like a cold, bitter wind tried to suck out my breath. That's all. Just bitterness and cold. It pretty much describes Samuel's personality."

Dropping his arms, Nate took a step back. "Maybe your gifts are warning you he's a threat, or maybe it's the cold chill of his death you're feeling."

"I have no clue, but I did see the way his face paled when I mentioned Leon. And that's my focus right now." Holly took in a shuddering breath and pasted on a fake confident smile. "Leon's outside with Harry. Let's go find him."

They retraced their steps and headed through the loading bay and out the back of the funeral home.

"About time you turned up. What have you been doing?" Harry swooped in and hovered in front of Holly. "You're pale. Are you getting sick? You taking your temperature? Keeping track?" The raven spun and flapped his wings in Nate's face. "What did you do?"

Holding his hands up, Nate pushed the raven back. He shook his head. "Not me. She touched the funeral director's hand and had trouble breathing. Nothing to do with me."

Holly checked her temperature with the back of her hand. "No fever. I'm fine." She lowered her hand. "Where's Leon?"

"Over by the angel monument you hate so much. I followed him for a while, but it was boring, so I've been sorta hovering. I saw him duck behind the angel monument for a while and I haven't seen him walk past, so it doesn't look like he's moved."

Grimacing, Holly nodded. "Thanks." She turned left and headed to a large stone angel with wings outspread.

"You don't like angels?" Nate kept pace.

"It's supposed to be the angel of death. It freaks me out. The statue has a supercilious smile that discombobulates me."

"Death isn't arrogant."

"How do you know that, Amnesia Boy? More returning memories?"

"Just a feeling."

"Whatever you feel, I still hate that statue." Holly spotted Leon, the gravedigger, leaning against the statue. "Leon."

The gravedigger stiffened. "Ms. Harrow. I thought you were off today."

"Oh, I am," Holly rushed to agree. "But I'm just clearing a few things off my plate before I enjoy the day. Did you hear about that janitor, Arnold Twigg? He's dead. Murdered."

"I don't know nothing about a dead guy." Leon shuffled his feet and refused to meet Holly's gaze.

"Really? I saw you talking to him at the hospital. And I'm pretty sure our temporary boss knows about you and Arnold too, and he's been seen hanging out with Twigg as well. Interesting group of friends you have," Holly pushed.

"Nothing to do with me. What Mr. Wood does on his own time is just that. His time. I'd stay away from him if I was you." Leon slapped his leg. "I got work to do now." Ignoring Holly, Leon headed off in the opposite direction.

"A man with demons on his mind and death in his soul." Harry fluttered his wings and landed on the angel's outstretched wing. "Of course, he digs graves, so he could also be suffering from a virulent plague. It's a fifty-fifty chance."

"Although I never want to agree with a taxidermy Viking raven, Leon definitely knows something," Nate agreed.

"And he warned me away from Samuel. I can feel another breaking and entering mission in my future." Searching her temporary boss's room at Mayweather Inn might just be the sleuthing break Holly needed...

THIRTEEN

"A stroke of luck that the pipes burst just as we needed Rose to leave the reception desk."

Holly snorted. "Elspeth says there's no such thing as coincidence. Just people carving their own path."

"That sounds more philosophical than I expected Elspeth to be."

"I think she found the saying on the back of a whiskey bottle." Holly gestured. "Samuel's room is just up here." The banshee angled her head around the corner and peeked into the hallway. "All clear." The duo casually strolled along toward the room.

"I can't believe I'm saying this but the allure of the dark, high adrenaline world of breaking and entering has paled."

"Yeah. You do get used to it. I'm just glad Harry elected to stay with the moped."

A twin set of giggles trickled down along the hallway and the two women, Ris and Patty, poked their dark heads around the wall near the back stairs of the inn.

Ris gave the duo a thumbs-up, then both women disappeared down the stairs.

"Those two enjoy chaos and mayhem more than Elspeth and that says a lot." Holly stopped in front of Samuel's room and pointed at the partially open door. She lowered her voice and whispered, "Looks like someone got here before us. Let's see what's going on." Holly slapped the door wide open, exposing a tall, skinny, blonde woman. "Callista."

Leon's girlfriend, spun, her hand holding a rolled-up wad of cash. She immediately went on the offensive. "Excuse me? It's rude to just barge into someone else's room. I should leave a complaint." She scowled at Holly and Nate and brazenly tucked the cash away in her pocket.

Nate leaned against the doorjamb, hazel eyes sparking. "Bold. Wants to lay a complaint when she's the one stealing cash from the occupant. Do you even know who's staying here?"

"Someone who owes me." Callista spat the words.

"I'm doing what I need to. To protect myself."

"Uh huh." Holly tucked her hands in her jeans' pockets and stood next to Nate. She hated searching other people's rooms, pawing through their belongings and their second-hand germs. At least Callista had saved her from decontamination. But looking around the room, it was clear that Samuel was immaculate. Except for the habit of leaving wads of cash around. Holly detoured back to the conversation. "And what about Leon? Are you protecting him too?"

Callista hissed, shaking her head. Her straight blonde hair swung and settled around her shoulders in a sheet of gold. "He's the one who got us involved. If he'd just shut his mouth, we'd be home and free. But no, he had to look for the money angle."

"And Samuel? Why raid his room?"

"You don't go back on a deal. I'm taking what's owed to me." Callista raced at Holly, sending her flying as she pushed her way out of the room.

Tight bands of warmth encircled Holly's waist and drew her against the nearest stable object...*Nate*. She fought the urge to squirm against his solid chest. "Good catch. But you can put me down now, so I can follow her."

"If I must." Nate sighed but released Holly.

"To the moped." Holly giggled as she raced down the back stairs of Mayweather Inn. Xandie was right, sleuthing could be fun. And Nate wasn't too bad either.

They reached the parking lot, but Callista had already disappeared.

"Hecate's snails. Too slow," Holly cursed. "Fine, it's a sign. We'll call it a day. We'll head up to the Library and fill everyone in on what we know so far."

"What do we know?"

"Enough that I have a new suspect list." Holly shoved her spare helmet at Nate. "Get a wriggle on, Amnesia Boy. I don't have all day."

"The way you drive, it'll take all day to get to the Library."

"Hey," Holly protested. "Library's only just up the hill past the inn. It's literally a five-minute drive away."

"Exactly." Nate slid his leg over the moped and patted the seat.

"Everyone's a backseat driver," Holly grumbled but slid in front of her passenger, squeaking when he wrapped arms around her waist, holding her tight. Good thing Harry wasn't here. He'd be dropping a barrage of snide comments. Holly pulled out onto the road, aiming for the Library. A non-descript black car with tinted windows pulled out behind them. Holly moved over to the side of the road, far enough for the car to pass if it needed to. But the vehicle stayed close behind them... *Too close.* "I think you'd better hold tight," Holly yelled over her shoulder.

"What's wrong?" Nate's grip tightened.

"That car is way too close for comfort." Holly gripped her moped's handlebars tight. A bead of sweat trickled its way along her spine, accompanied by a familiar itch. *Not now! Not now!*

The car suddenly pulled out and levelled with her moped. The banshee stiffened her spine. The turn-off for the Library was only just ahead. They'd be fine. They just had to get there safely.

The car shot forward and then pulled back to the side of the moped again. This time the driver angled closer, pushing Holly farther and farther to the shadowed edge of the road and the deep ditch next to it.

Holly's moped wobbled as she fought to gain traction on the loose gravel. The car shoved closer, and this time Holly couldn't control the moped and it tipped to the side and slid off into the ditch, sending its riders flying. Holly had no time to even squeak as the ground sped toward her. She closed her eyes as the impact caused her body to bounce. Thankfully,

she always made sure she wore a helmet, or scrambled senses would have been the outcome. Her vison
went black as she heard a revving noise from the road
as the car took off.

"Holly? Holly? Are you okay?"

Nate's voice sounded from above the banshee,
and she groaned, pushing her body half off the
ground. "I think we should both be glad I drive at a
snail's pace."

"Here." Nate helped Holly stand and swiped at
the mud on the visor of her helmet. "Better." Nate
released the banshee to stand on her own feet. "Are
you okay?"

Holly winced at a sudden jab of pain in one of
her legs. "Not so much, no." But at least she had her
vision back thanks to Nate wiping the mud away.
Holly squeaked as she gingerly put her weight on her
left foot.

"Here. Hold on to me." Nate grabbed Holly's arm
and wound it around his waist. "Lean on me. I'm
pretty sure the car's gone now." Following orders,
Holly allowed Nate to take most of the weight as
they climbed back up onto the empty road.

"My poor moped. May she rest in peace." No
wonder they'd fallen into the ditch. Her pretty silver
moped's back wheel still sat on the road. Unfortu-

nately, the rest had landed elsewhere. "Are you okay? Were you hurt?" An urgency gripped Holly as she peered up at Nate's muddy face. He'd already taken off his helmet. Following suit, Holly managed to pry her helmet off and drop it to the side of the road. How horrible was she? Whining about her poor moped before checking her passenger for injuries? *Way to be compassionate, banshee.*

"I'm fine. I'm more worried about you. You're bleeding." He nodded at Holly's torn jeans.

Holly followed his gaze to her tender left leg and a large tear in her jeans. Red seeped through, soaking the material around the tear. She wavered on her feet as her vision tunneled, dark creeping in when she focused on the blood. Nausea rolled in her stomach, gathering momentum.

"Whoa there, Holly. Breathe through it. You're okay." Nate rubbed Holly's back.

Her vision cleared as she concentrated. "Obviously blood doesn't agree with me. Especially my own. And think of all the germs in the mud." She shuddered. "I'm doubly glad Harry isn't here, or he'd tell me that gangrene would set in and the healers would have to amputate my leg." She paused. "How long does gangrene take to set in?"

"I'm pretty sure you'll be fine. Where's the

Library?"

Holly pointed out a driveway just up the hill. "We're literally in front of her property. Lucky."

"Luck is not the word for it. Well, come on, banshee. We need to treat your leg before it falls off." Nate swung Holly into his arms, settling her before striding across the road.

"Hey." Holly thumped Nate's chest. "You said I'd be fine."

"You never know." He winked and chuckled.

Holly closed her eyes for a moment as she nestled against her personal heater. She must've drifted off, because the next thing the banshee knew, liquid fire bathed her leg. "Ouch. Why is my heater torturing me?" She opened her eyes to spot her cousin, Lila, pouring liquid over the wound. "The baker's learned torture methods?"

Lila rolled her eyes. "Please, we're Harrow. We learn torture techniques at Elspeth's knobbly knees. Every time she opens her mouth, it's torture." Lila leaned back and capped the bottle. "It's just a graze. Your leg is safe from the hacksaw."

Holly glared accusingly at Nate, who was sponging mud from his clothing. "You told her about the gangrene? *Seriously?* What about what happens on the mission stays on the mission?"

"Don't look at me. You were mumbling about gangrene while you were out of it."

"Gangrene is a serious concern unless you have a sneaky volva who can heal the wound." Harry flapped his wings from his perch on Xandie's heavy wooden desk in the Library. "The banshee's the only one marked and yet the man with no past is only concerned with cleaning mud. He has no bruises or scratches. Is this not unusual to anyone else?" The raven snapped his beak at Nate.

"In Point Muse? Not even close." Xandie swiped a towel over Holly's arm, cleaning mud away. "Zach's on the way. He wanted to check out the accident scene first." Xandie amended her words. "After we told him you're okay. I think he's bringing Elspeth."

"Oh, joy. Another lecture." Holly eased back into the comfortable couch. "Someone ran us off the road. The car had tinted windows, so we couldn't see who it was. But it followed us from Mayweather Inn. The same place where we found Callista, Leon's girl-friend, stealing cash from Samuel Wood's room."

"Your boss?"

"Temporary boss. She said she was only taking what he owed her." Holly broke off as the door swung open and hit the wall with a bang.

Elspeth stood framed in the doorway; arms crossed over her yellow velour jogging suit. The wicked witch wore a clashing orange mohawk wig. "No one is allowed to take a Harrow out except for me." She thumped her bony chest before snapping her fingers. "Kit, now."

Zach popped up behind Elspeth and handed her a small black bag.

The wicked witch stomped toward the banshee and yanked out a green velvet bag. Reaching in, she snatched a handful of sparkling dust and sprinkled it over Holly's leg wound. An itching spread over her leg, and Holly watched as the skin sealed, leaving behind a pink line. "I hate saying this...but thank you, Elspeth."

"I'll add it to your bill." Elspeth waved away the thanks. She paced up and down the length of the Library. "How dare someone target a Harrow. This needs a response. Maximum carnage, maximum mayhem."

"Why don't we all calm down?" Zach pointed to Holly and Nate. "What happened?"

"We surprise Callista stealing money from Samuel's room at the inn. She was too fast for us to follow. So, we left to come here, and a car ran us off the road." Holly held up a hand. "Before you ask, the windows were tinted, and we couldn't see who the driver was."

"Curses. Foiled," Elspeth growled and stamped her foot. A large crack of thunder sounded over the Library, and a sudden burst of wind and rain hammered the windows.

Everyone stared at the wicked witch. She shrugged. "Timing is everything. It wasn't me. Just a normal storm."

"This time." Lila sniffed. "I checked with Dad to see if he'd heard anything."

Lila's father was captain of security for Hades, God of the underworld, and a poker buddy, and both men loved a good gossip. Holly stretched her legs cautiously before swinging them off the couch.

Nate was instantly at her side to help her stand. Harry flapped and flew over the top of Nate's head.

"Hands off. It's your fault she was injured. This is all connected to you. I'd stake my feathers on it."

"Calm down, bird." Holly pushed both man and bird away and tried a few steps. Finding nothing but stiffness, she moved a few more paces before starting a lap around the edges of the Library to work away her kinks. Lightning flashed intermittently through the uncovered windows. "Carry on."

"Thanks, your Majesty." Lila wrinkled her nose

but continued, "Apparently there was a breakout from Tartarus, where Hades holds his prisoners."

Xandie rolled her eyes. "Wouldn't be the first time. He really needs a prison security overhaul."

"This time, there were two prisoners. One's a serial murderer and the other a blackmailer. Dad thinks it might have been an inside job as well. Hades is frothing about it."

Holly paused on her lap of the Library in front of one of the windows. Lightning continued to illuminate the darkening landscape. A large, black storm cloud swallowed the light of the late afternoon. A flash of something or someone darting behind the garden statues of the nine Muses caught Holly's attention. Another figure joined the first near the statues. "There are two people in the back near the statues."

"What?" Nate strode to the window, Zach glued to his side. With a shared glance, they both headed outside.

"About time we had some action." Elspeth clapped her hands and followed the men.

"Should we stop her?" Xandie gnawed on her lip.

"Are you high on witch weed?" Holly widened her eyes. "No one stops the wicked witch from doing what she wants. Besides, we have more issues at hand."

"Like finding a murderer before another body turns up. This one with a Harrow attached to it," Lila agreed.

"Do you think Hades' prisoners are the ones we're looking for?" Xandie peered out the window, searching for her husband.

"You know what Elspeth says about coincidences." Holly fluffed her helmet-flattened hair, while musing on the problem of the escaped prisoners. *A murderer and a blackmailer?* Blackmail seemed up Leon's alley, but murder? The loud thump of a book slamming open on Xandie's desk jerked Holly away from her musings.

"Message incoming from the Library." Xandie rushed to the appointment book that now lay open on the desk. A thick, black scrawl appeared, letter by letter, on the page. Xandie read it aloud. "Message from the Elysian Fields Funeral Home receptionist. Callista now wishes to meet you at her place tomorrow morning after her shift at the hospital. She has information she's willing to share." Xandie looked at Holly. "There's an address on the harbor. Looks like you have a morning meeting."

This is just the break a sleuthing banshee needs...

FOURTEEN

"At least this time we're invited and don't need to break and enter. No chance of ending up in police cells and catching some virulent disease."

Holly poked Harry in the stomach. "I keep telling you. It's never breaking, just entering, when we have a skeleton key."

"And don't get me started on the number of germs human bones carry."

"Hey, that's my Great-Aunt Rose you're maligning, or was it Great-Great-Aunt Rose? I always forget." Holly paused. "Although now that I stop and think about it, you're probably right." She screwed up her face. "Maybe you should suggest a decontamination bath for the key when we get back to Harrow House."

"Maybe we should focus on your meeting?" Nate rapped on the door of Callista's smart looking townhouse. The door immediately creaked open. "I'm guessing that's probably not a good sign?"

"Not so much, no." Holly sighed, then mentally pulled up her big girl panties and stepped inside. "Callista?" the banshee called out. "You wanted to meet up?" Chaos met Holly's gaze when she stepped into a small living room. Clothing lay everywhere, draped over furniture, the table, and the floor. Two open suitcases, partially filled, sat next to the couch. Matching throw pillows from the couch decorated the floor. "Does this look searched or like a case of bad housekeeping or frantic packing?"

"Combination of the three? I take that back. This seems more like frantic packing to me."

"Why?"

"She's got things in color piles. That seems more like packing than tidiness or searching."

Amnesia Boy was observant. "Good point. I'll take the bedroom." Heading upstairs and avoiding discarded shoe piles, Holly turned left into a similarly chaotic bedroom. "Girl has a shopping problem." A large number of multi-colored sweaters lay dead center on the large queen size bed. Popping her head into the bathroom, Holly spotted a complex range of expensive beauty lotions and potions. She picked up a pink, crystal bottle with her mom's shop logo on it. "Ever-fresh skin mist." She made a note to speak to her mother about Callista's buying habits. Harry dropped down on Holly's shoulder.

"Vanity. A deadly sin that will take down the most pious of people." He clucked. "Although, some kind of volva potion or lotion might help your dry skin problems." He poked his beak at Holly's cheek.

"Hey." She flicked the raven's head. "My skin's fine." But she surreptitiously stroked a finger along her cheek, just in case.

"She's obsessed with beauty potions." Nate held out a handful of invoices. "It amazes me how people become so obsessed with appearance."

Holly glared at Harry. "What he said."

"For once, I don't disagree with the blank mind."

"Be nice, bird." Holly grabbed some of the invoices and read through them. "Wow. She racked up quite a debt for some creams that hide wrinkles."

"And quite a few from your mother." Nate held up another handful with Winifred Harrow's name stamped across the top. "She owed at least a thousand dollars and was on her second notice to pay. But it looks like she cleared all her debts off yesterday."

Handing the receipts back to Nate, Holly

headed downstairs to Callista's living room. Harry lifted off her shoulders and zoomed around the room.

"I bet she used that big wad of cash she stole from Samuel to pay off her debts."

"Then decided to skip town. Maybe?" Nate glanced around the messy room again. "Thinking about it, this room definitely looks like someone packed in a panic."

"But is she running from Samuel because of the stolen cash? Or from somebody else?"

Harry stiffened and dropped to a side table, wobbling toward a black lamp with a large lampshade. "Alert. Someone is outside. I suggest hiding quick smart, banshee."

Squeaking, Holly glanced around for a hiding spot.

"In here." Nate hooked a hand around Holly's elbow and towed her toward a skinny broom closet. He opened the door and pushed the banshee inside, crowding in behind her.

"It's too tight. We'll suffocate," Holly hissed as she tried to hold herself away from Nate. Futile gesture, as there was no room to move. Her whole body was plastered against his lean length. "And oxygen. What if there isn't enough in here?" Her breathing sped up. They could die here. Her family would find their bodies squeezed together in a broom closet and she didn't even like cleaning.

"Relax. There's plenty of air." Nate reached a hand up and adjusted the slats slightly open at the top of the door so they had airflow and a restricted view of the living room. "See? Airflow. Now hush. If the raven's right, someone's coming."

Holly grumbled but subsided and took a tiny breath in, testing his theory of plenty of air. Nate's musky scent, with hints of rich, deep earth, wrapped around the banshee. Warmth spread through the pit of Holly's stomach like a bushfire out of control, burning up into her throat and erupting into her fiery, pink cheeks. Thank goodness the closet was dark, or she'd never hear the end of it from Nate... *Or Harry.* "Is Harry hiding?"

"Under a lamp. He looks like a tacky decoration." A click sounded as the door to Callista's townhouse eased open.

Nate stiffened and Holly peeked through the slat as a black, caped figure glided in. Bobbing in and out of view, the figure drifted around the room, obviously, searching for something... *Or someone.* The figure finished walking through the townhouse and stood for a few moments in the center of the living room before exiting silently again.

Holly sagged against Nate. His lean strength supported her. After waiting for a few moments, the banshee opened the closet door, stumbled out, and fanned herself. "Good hiding place, but tight fit."

"Felt good to me." Nate winked and strolled over to the black lamp. He tapped on the lampshade. "The intruder's gone. You're safe to unfreeze and whine."

The lampshade shook, and Harry hopped out from underneath, flapping his wings. "I do not whine. I actively voice my opinion. And my opinion is we need to leave before the killer finds us again."

"We weren't the only ones the caped figure was looking for. I think Callista realized she was in danger and bolted. And it probably saved her life."

"Considering what we just saw, you're probably right." Nate glanced around the townhouse. "I suggest we head to Winifred's potion and lotions store and quiz her on Callista. She may have some insight."

"A visit with Mom it is." *And, hopefully, no jumping into tight spaces with appealing men will be needed...*

"And this one has monkey poop in it. Leaves such a glistening glow on the skin. Try it."

Holly avoided the test bottle her mother waved in her face. "It sounds so appealing, but I'll have to pass right now. We're here on sleuthing business."

"You really should reconsider, sweetie. You're looking a bit dry." Winifred pointed to the side of Holly's face.

"Ha." Harry bobbed his head up and down from his perch on a shelf over Winifred's front counter. "I told you so. You should take the volva's advice. I wouldn't because I don't trust any volva, but you should. *Dry. Dry.*" The raven cawed the last word with a mocking tilt of his head.

"It's wise to be cautious of witches, but I'm fairly sure Holly's mother is a safe choice." Nate held up a blue crystal, spray bottle and sniffed it experimentally.

"Good choice. That's blooming jasmine. Good for liver disease, dysentery, relaxation. And also heightens sexual desire." Winifred beamed. "Plus, it smells amazing."

Holly closed her eyes. "Do we need to talk about this right now?"

Winifred rounded on her daughter, hands on curvy hips. "Just because you find it uncomfortable doesn't mean the rest of us shouldn't talk about it. You'd be amazed the number of people who need help in the sexual arena."

Nate cleared his throat and carefully placed the bottle back on the shelf. "Thankfully, I'm fairly sure I'm fine in that area, but I promise to consult you if the problem ever arises... *So to speak.*" Pink spread across his cheeks, and he avoided looking at Winifred and Holly.

Harry hooted. "Never too early to admit to a problem, boy."

Glaring at the taxidermy raven, Nate took a threatening step forward.

Butting in before feathers flew, Holly pinned her mother with an interrogative stare. "What do you know about Callista, Leon's girlfriend?" She flattened a few invoices on the glass counter and showed them to her mother.

Peering at the invoices, Winifred nodded. "Callista Demos has an obsession with staying young and beautiful. Which for a potions and lotions store is great news. Except she's a lousy bill payer." Holly's mother shook her head. "I never should have opened a tab for her, but it's hard to say no when a customer begs you."

"She owed you a lot of money?"

"One thousand dollars. She just paid the entire bill off yesterday. Rushed in with a heap of cash."

The same cash stolen from Samuel's room at the inn. "How did she seem?"

"Frantic, dear. Normally, she's calm. Yesterday, Callista seemed distracted. She rushed in and out without buying anything. That's highly unusual for her." Winifred smoothed her daughter's hair back into its shiny, chin-length shape. "There you go, dear. Now you look lovely."

"Thanks, Mom." Holly forced herself not to look at Nate in case he was laughing at her mother's maternal urges. "Something spooked her. She was running."

Nate nodded, agreeing with Holly's assessment. "Did Callista ever tell you about her background? Where she came from and why she picked Point Muse?"

Winifred settled on a carved, wooden stool behind her counter. "She let a few things drop, like she didn't pick Point Muse. Leon did."

"They were a couple before Point Muse?"

Grimacing, Winifred wobbled her hand. "Kind of. She implied they'd been a couple for a long time but separated for some reason. And Leon had been away. But now that he was back, they were together."

"Mom, do you know why Leon chose Point Muse?"

"Callista wouldn't say. Just that he was following the money." Winifred looked downcast. "That isn't very helpful, is it?"

"More than you think, Ms. Harrow." Nate reached over and squeezed Holly's mother's hand.

Winifred perked up and beamed. "Thank you, dear. I do remember something else."

"Yes?" Holly prodded. The Harrow gene for drama was never more evident than when under interrogation.

"Callista visited the shop last week with Leon. He waited outside while she shopped. And that snooty Mr. Wood accosted him outside and had words."

Samuel again. Always popping up where he isn't wanted. "Could you hear the conversation?"

"No. But there was handwaving. I asked Callista if Leon was okay, but she brushed it off. Called it a business disagreement. Their disagreement finished as soon as Callista joined them. But neither Samuel nor Leon looked very happy with each other." Winifred wiggled on her chair. "That was helpful, wasn't it? I helped you sleuth."

"Yeah. Thanks, Mom. You helped." Holly

needed to fit her clues together, but she was slowly getting a picture and a suspect list. Leon had been separated from Callista for a period, then had probably followed somebody else to Point Muse. Someone connected to a business scheme... *In other words, blackmail.* Holly had a feeling Leon was one of Hades' escaped prisoners. But how did Samuel figure into the equation?

The door to Winifred's shop swung open, and Xandie stood panting in the doorway. Her normally frizzy, shoulder-length hair lay plastered against her head and her chest heaved up and down. "We've got a problem."

"No," Holly wailed and leapt up, slapping a hand over her cousin's mouth. "Don't say it. You'll jinx us. We can pretend you weren't here."

"Too late, dear. We all heard it. Why don't you let your cousin go before you suffocate her?"

Xandie flicked her tongue out and licked Holly's palm, causing her to squeal and drop her hand.

Holly wiped the hand on her jeans. "Do you know how many germs a human mouth has?" She glared at Xandie.

Xandie held up her hands. "It's not my fault you tried to muzzle me. I have important news; you can't silence the truth." Xandie pumped a hand into the air. She lowered her hand awkwardly as everyone stared. "Sorry, too much time around Elspeth."

"News, dear?" Winifred smiled at her niece.

"Right. That nurse you found stealing. She's in the hospital. Zach was called out to a car accident. The car's brakes failed as it was heading out of town. Apparently, it's Callista." Xandie smirked. "See? My news was important." She snapped her fingers. "And Lila said her dad and Hades are planning to visit too. You might get more information out of them when they arrive."

Maybe she'd find out who helped them escape from the underworld. And were they still helping them? For now, a trip to the worst place in Point Muse was called for... *The hospital.*

FIFTEEN

"Hospitals are germ incubators." Holly drew closer to Nate as they trudged down the hallway to Callista's room.

"Big, brave banshee scared of germs?" Nate teased, a twinkle in his hazel eyes.

"Do you have any idea the percentage of diseases a hospital has laying around on any given day?" Holly shivered. "You go in and you don't come out."

"A banshee with a germ phobia. Who would have guessed?" Nate stifled a chuckle. "Is that the reason you left Harry behind with Winifred? Because he's a germ hater too?"

"That and he whines." Holly glanced around. The hospital didn't seem quite as chaotic as the last time they were there. "Does it seem quieter to you?"

Nate gave a cursory glance around. "Maybe the hospital is just coping better?"

"They have wards set up now. Any dead alive patients are immediately admitted and sedated. They might be technically dead, but medication still works." Zach Braun, Xandie's husband and the police chief, stood outside a private hospital room.

The bear shifter looked exhausted. His sandy-colored hair stood up in all directions, and the bags under his eyes had their own zip codes. "Married life does not look like it's agreeing with you."

"The problem isn't married life. It's people not staying dead," Zach growled. "I hear Callista Demos is of interest to you. This about Nate's memory?"

Holly nibbled on the corner of her lip. "I think the temporary funeral director is involved. Which makes sense as we found this one there." She jabbed her finger at her sleuthing partner. "And Samuel and Leon are definitely connected. Arnold Twigg most likely blackmailed one or both. And Callista's Leon's girlfriend. She's either a suspect or at risk because of her knowledge. We aren't sure yet." Holly ran out of breath. "I think that's it." She waved a hand. "Oops, I forgot. There's also a shadowy, caped killer hanging around who was looking for Callista." Holly beamed, proud of her recall.

"Well." Zach massaged his forehead and then stepped to the side, allowing Holly and Nate to see the tubed figure of Callista, lying still in a hospital bed. "Someone found her. At least found her brakes. The brakes were tampered with. She ran into a tree but is alive. In a coma, but still alive."

"What's her prognosis?" Nate perused the silent woman.

"They think she'll come out of it, but the doctors have no clue when. The healers have dealt with her more serious injuries, but they want to see if she comes out of the coma by herself without intervention first."

Nate nodded. "Makes sense. Some healing practices have serious side-effects, especially those associated with brain injuries. Healing would be the last resort."

"You seem knowledgeable about healing practices." Zach considered the man in front of him suspiciously.

"I get flashes." Nate shrugged. "I have feelings, and I read a lot."

"Can we focus back on Callista?" Holly grimaced as she speared a glance around her. "I'd like to get out of here as soon as possible."

"Callista listed Leon as her next of kin. But I

can't get a hold of him. He seems to have disappeared. Any idea where I might find him?"

"At work. Or at least he's meant to be."

"I checked. He didn't turn up. I checked here at the hospital too, but he seems to have disappeared."

"Hmm." Holly started pacing in front of the door. People milled around, including Ris and Patty, who stood in a waiting room opposite Callista's hospital room, chatting to a cute doctor. Ris waved at Holly when she noticed her watching. Huffing, the banshee spun back to Zach. "He isn't at Callista's or Mom's shop because we just checked there."

"If you see him, don't approach. Just call it in and one of us will come straight out." He fixed Holly with a stern stare. "Lila and Xandie are unable to listen, but I'm hoping you have more sense."

Widening her eyes, Holly nodded. "I'm definitely the most sensible Harrow. You can count on me."

"Why don't I believe you? I need to get back to the station, but I'm leaving Melody inside with Callista, just in case. Stay safe." He waved over his shoulder and headed off.

"Seriously? *You're* the most sensible of all the Harrows?" Nate stared incredulously at the banshee.

Holly smirked. "I'm the most sensible of my cousins. With the exception of Liam, since he's a deputy now and works for the other side, aka law enforcement," she amended. A mythical male Harrow had popped up a while ago with his grandfather, Edgar, Elspeth's youngest brother. Edgar could be as frustrating as her grandmother, but Liam was a decent Harrow. Much to Elspeth and Edgar's regret.

"What now?"

She crooked a finger and pointed down the hallway. "Now you follow me, and we regroup at Lila's bakery. Food helps you think and work out what to do next." Holly headed toward the nearby nurse's station. She'd make sure the hospital contacted her *if* Callista came out of the coma. Holly ground to a halt when she spotted Samuel *"Woo Woo"* Wood in his Victorian garb, holding tight to a top hat, standing next to the nurse's station, arguing.

"I can tell you, madam, the Elysian Fields Funeral Home does not make mistakes. We were called to pick up a Callista Demos for burial. Obviously, burial indicates death, ergo, Callista Demos is dead. So, please direct me to her room, so we can conduct our business."

"As *I* stated, sir, I cannot divulge patients' room numbers. But I can tell you, the patient, Callista Demos, is not deceased." The tired-looking nurse slammed a file onto her desk and glared at the funeral director. "Don't make me call security."

"This hospital had better prepare itself for a hefty lawsuit. My funeral home prides itself on top-notch service," Samuel pompously declared.

Holly snorted. The horsey snort came out louder than she'd expected. She couldn't help it. *Ah well...in for a penny.* "Top-notch service? Like burying a client alive? Or picking up clients from the hospital when they haven't even died yet?"

Samuel spun and his grip on his hat loosened. The top hat hit the ground and rolled to Nate's feet.

Leaning down, Nate picked up the hat and dusted it off. He held it out to Samuel. "I find doing your research and carrying out an accurate determination of aliveness tends to derail any litigation."

"This is none of your business." Samuel snatched the hat out of Nate's hand.

Whoa. No one insults Amnesia Boy but me, and maybe Elspeth. Holly slammed her hands on her hips and shot her temporary boss a poisonous glance. "But the funeral home *is* my business, and I've seen Callista. She's not deceased. I think you should stop verbally haranguing the poor nurse. There's obviously been a mistake made on your side."

With a hiss, Samuel spun on Holly. "The only

mistake was hiring a banshee and a Harrow. But don't worry, I can rectify that right now. Ms. Harrow, you're fired. The funeral business needs serious-minded people. Not dilettantes who have a morbid fascination with the dead. You're out." Samuel slapped his top hat on his head.

"Excuse you? You can't do that. You're only a fill-in funeral director. You're not even my full-time boss." A tornado spun in the bottom of Holly's stomach and a vice closed around the banshee's throat.

"Your bosses gave me full power to manage the home. I can certainly fire you. And now I'm going to complete my job and sort out this mess." He stomped along the hallway, fists clenched, frock coat tails flying.

"That... That..." Red swept up into Holly's cheeks, blazing away like two indignant beacons. She clenched her fist and opened and closed her mouth. Speechless. *For once.*

Nate wrapped his arm around her. "Maybe we should get you to the bakery. Lila can ply you with sugared goods and let you explode. Internalizing emotions is a bad health choice."

"I'm so sorry." The wide-eyed nurse shook her head. "He just wouldn't listen. I kept telling him she was still alive. He was so sure she was deceased; he wouldn't listen. Kept ranting about a mistake and needing the room number to correct it."

The nurse's words drove Holly back from the brink of emotional eruption. She was right. Samuel had looked sure that Callista had died. How could he be so positive unless he had something to do with her accident?

"Don't be sorry. I'm sure Holly will be reinstated as soon as her normal employers are back from leave. I'll make sure of it." Nate nodded to the nurse and steered Holly along the hallway, heading out of the hospital.

The banshee allowed herself to be towed outside as metaphorical ants itched along her arms. Silver fog seeped along the edges of her vision as her banshee blood ignited.

"Lila's bakery?"

Holly slowly took a step away from Nate's guiding arm and faced him. "We need to get to the funeral home. Search Samuel's office and locker." Her eyes flickered between silver and amber. Her voice lowered in timber as her banshee gifts took hold. "Death. Death is waiting at the funeral home, and we need to see the gift it left us..."

Holly scratched her arm. "I said I was fine."

"You also said death was waiting at the funeral home," Nate reminded her.

"Can't help what I say when the banshee takes control."

"The banshee doesn't take control. *You* are the banshee. Death triggers your gifts. That's all."

"I don't want to talk about it." Holly clenched her teeth. Most banshees bonded with a family when they were young, but some found their bond when they were older. Her dad's banshee gifts had bonded with another family when he was an adult, and he'd left when she was young. They talked every week, and he did his best to help with her banshee gifts over the phone. But it wasn't the same as learning in person. She was still feeling her way through her gifts. It was more of a minefield than a pleasant stroll.

"Fine." Nate threw his hands up. "But there's a reason your gifts are unpredictable. You need to accept your banshee blood and acknowledge you're in control. No one else. Just you."

"In Elspeth's famous words, I acknowledge you need to shut your trap." Holly gritted her teeth and nodded at Dolly, the funeral home's troll receptionist. Hopefully, news of her firing hadn't spread through town already.

"Oh. My. Goddess. Mr. Wood rang me. I can't believe he fired you." The receptionist spread her large, green-tinged troll hands wide and waved them in the air in front of her face, air drying the puce-colored nail polish.

Holly rolled her eyes. So much for her hope that no one knew. "Yep. I protested when he tried to pick up a coma patient from the hospital."

Dolly frowned. Her thick, bushy, beetle brows wiggled like fat caterpillars on her face. "But he didn't get any pick-up orders from the hospital today. Since dead people started walking around, our burial lists have shrunk to almost nothing. Although..." Dolly flipped through her paperwork, gingerly making sure not to mar her polish. "We did get another John Doe schedule for burial a little while ago. I've been looking for Leon everywhere, but I guess he decided not to show up again today. Doug and Dave had to do the digging."

Holly choked and stared, horrified, at Nate. *Another John Doe?* What were the odds another live burial had occurred? "What's the plot number?"

"Section two A, plot twelve." Dolly glanced around. "Don't worry about your job either. I saw

Samuel carrying some boxes out to his car early this morning before he headed out. I think he's planning on leaving. Which must mean the big bosses will be back soon." Dolly sat back, smiling with jagged teeth. "Think of your firing as a vacation. You'll be back working in no time." She beamed.

"Okay, thanks, Dolly. Got to go now." Holly grabbed Nate's arm and towed him out the door and around the back. "We need to get to the plot."

Nate inhaled. "You think we have another live burial?"

"I think we had. *Had*. We need to see what Samuel's buried... Or who." Holly rushed through the different sections of the cemetery, searching for a specific plot. "Over here."

"How do you know where to go?"

"Our cemetery is laid out in different sections. If you know where each section begins, all you do is count plots from the start of that section. Look." Holly pointed to a freshly dug grave. "That's plot twelve. Quick." She rushed forward and frantically scraped the dirt away.

"Uh, boss? What you doing?" Doug, Dolly's brother, one of Holly's expert team members, stood on the side of the grave, scratching the back of his thick neck.

"Not your boss anymore. And I think we might have a live burial."

Doug shook his head. "Nah. Mr. Wood signed off and delivered the casket to us. It's all good."

"Would you all just help me?" Holly screeched.

Nate squatted and dug in the dirt. "I think it's too late, Holly. Remember what you said? Death waits at the funeral home?"

"I don't care what I said. We have to try." Holly scrabbled furiously through the dirt.

"You better move then, boss." Doug flexed his troll muscles. "You need an expert for this." He made quick work of the dirt and uncovered a plain brown casket. He used his shovel and cracked the casket slightly open.

Shoving past the troll, Holly wrenched the lid open and fell back, shrieking when she uncovered the occupant... Leon. Mouth open, full of bark and dirt.

"Man. This isn't good." Doug sidestepped away and then grimaced when he heard a noise behind them.

Ignoring her troll workmate, Holly dropped her head into her hands. "I wasn't quick enough."

Nate crouched next to the banshee. "You can't change people's life choices. Leon was always headed toward this. You can't blame yourself. You didn't put him in the ground. Someone else did."

"Boss, I found these two peeping toms watching you." Dave, Doug's brother, dumped two flailing young women at the side of the grave.

Holly took a deep breath and pushed herself to her feet, nodding her thanks before focusing on the women. "What a surprise. Ris and Patty. You seem to have your curious noses everywhere. Did you follow us from the hospital? Are you a part of this?"

Ris shook her head wildly. "This wasn't us. Not our thing. I swear..."

Patty agreed. "We like mayhem, but that..." She trailed off and pointed at Leon's body. "That's some freaky crap. Who knew Point Muse could get so crazy?"

Nate growled, hands fisted at his sides. "People are dying."

"Some people." Ris winked at Nate.

"Stop messing around," Nate thundered at Little Miss Pixie. "Death isn't a joke."

Why did this conversation suddenly sound personal? What else was going on here? Holly's gaze pinged between the three arguers.

"Neither is being grabbed by trolls." Patty rubbed her arms and glared.

Holly gave up on the argument. She looked down at Leon. This had to stop. She needed to know what the heck was going on. "Whatever thing you three have going on, it needs to be tabled. We have another murder and a cop to call."

Ris and Patty drew themselves upright, babbling together and waving their arms at Nate, proclaiming their innocence and the unnecessary need for police.

Holly clapped her hands. "That's enough. We're calling the cops. This has to be done properly." Holly just knew this meant another round of sitting on cold, hard metal chairs being questioned. But she didn't have a choice. As long as it didn't end with Elspeth storming the station with stink bombs...*again*.

SIXTEEN

"Where was my Elspeth Harrow rescue-from-jail special? Did you forget where the police station was?" Holly glowered as she stomped into the bakery the next morning. Her smooth brown bob stuck up in multiple directions. To add insult to injury, Amnesia Boy had nary a hair out of place. Life wasn't fair. Even her shirt was creased to within an inch of its life and her jeans were marked and stained. Holly ducked behind the bakery counter, grabbed a packet of wipes, and proceeded to decontaminate herself.

Elspeth leaned against the counter and toasted her granddaughter with a mug of coffee. "You only get one get out of jail free visit from me."

"You lie," Holly hissed at the wicked witch.

"What about all the times you rescued Xandie? *Huh? Huh?*" Holly raised her voice.

"She's my favorite. The most likely to give me great grandchildren first. They might be part furry but it's the Harrow blood that counts."

"Meyers blood and Braun blood," Xandie muttered under her breath. She pushed a plate of decadent brownies at her cousin. "You're hangry. You need a sugar hit."

Holly stomped to a chair and collapsed. She grabbed a brownie and tore into it, gnashing her teeth as she stared around at the still quiet bakery.

"Hangry. I recognize the symptoms." Colin popped his head out from underneath the table. "Feed the anger and she'll calm down. Happens to me all the time."

Harry swept in and came to a stop on the back of the chair. "Your shadow has disappeared, little banshee."

Holly jerked her head. "My shadow is currently bickering with two annoying peeping Thomasinas... *again.*"

"It wasn't our fault. We keep telling you this." Ris stomped into the bakery. Her black pixie cut stood up in clumps like Holly's.

"We were lurking, not killing. *Lurking.*" Patty

joined her sister and glared at Nate, her black braid swinging like a displeased cat's tail.

"Lurking? In a graveyard? Near a dead body?" Nate raised his voice.

"Technically, there's lots of dead bodies in a graveyard." Ris high-fived her sister and let out a cackle reminiscent of Elspeth's. The sound of metal hitting the ground, accompanied by the tinkling of glass smashing, filled the bakery.

"Elspeth." Hester, Lila's brownie employee, slammed out of the kitchen, holding a carton of milk. "Quit the hag act. My pots are dented, glasses are broken, and our milk has soured."

"It wasn't me."

The cappuccino machine let out a high-pitched squeal, along with a massive vent of steam.

"Elspeth Harrow. Don't you dare break my bakery," Lila roared.

"*It. Wasn't. Me,*" Elspeth bellowed back, pointing an electric-blue painted finger at her granddaughter. "And if everyone keeps yelling at me, I'll Taser the lot of you."

Nate spun and faced the two young women. "If it isn't Elspeth, then it's probably you two. So, cut it out. This is a place of business."

"Stop yelling at us."

"We can't help it."

The bakery door opened and an older man, with a gray-streaked beard and a dark brown, buzz cut hairdo, along with hulking muscles clothed in a smart tailored suit, strode in. His hazel eyes twinkled. "What kind of chaos are my girls causing this time?"

"Dad."

"Daddy."

The girls hurried over to their father and latched on in a three-way hug.

"Shadows," Holly murmured. Her skin itched and she absentmindedly scratched at the skin.

The older man looked at Holly and winked. "Apologies. My girls are high-spirited and very curious. Comes from being the babies of the family."

Elspeth sashayed toward the man and fluffed her baby pink, Shirley Temple style, corkscrew curly wig. "We know all about high spirits. We're Harrows."

Holly's eyes grew round, and she stared, horrified, at Xandie, who'd just covered her eyes. Was their wicked witch grandmother flirting? With a stranger? *In public?*

After detangling himself from his daughters, he took hold of Elspeth's hand and bowed over it.

"Elspeth Harrow, I presume? Your reputation precedes you."

Tittering, Elspeth winked. "Hopefully, it's all bad. And you are?"

He straightened and released his hold on the witch's hand. "I'm Rebus and you obviously know my daughters, Ris and Patty."

"They've been stalking the town and lurking around dead bodies. And we had to listen to them yapping at the police station last night. Not to mention, all the chaos of power outages, broken glass, and blocked plumbing." Holly glared at the girls, as if it was their fault.

Rebus quirked a bushy eyebrow. "Girls?"

"We aren't doing anything wrong... Well, not much," Patty amended.

"We just wanted to check out Point Muse before you and Mom turned up. Plus, we could check on big bro. He's been too quiet lately. We were worried."

Ris tried for a virtuous expression and both the girls blinked their eyes innocently at their father.

Sighing, Rebus turned to a silent Nate. "What have your sisters really been doing?"

"What?" Holly shot out of her chair, nearly colliding with Lila as she placed a plate of lemon bars on the table.

"No." Nate winced and put a hand to the back of his head. "No way are they my sisters."

"Your mother would dispute that." Rebus frowned. "What's going on here? You really don't remember your family?"

"I found him in a coffin at my funeral home, tied up in a silver chain forged by Hephaestus. He had a head injury."

"I healed him." Elspeth beamed, dentures on show.

"For some reason, the healing didn't fix his memory though. He has amnesia."

Harry took to the air and divebombed Nate's dark hair, ruffling the curls. "So, he claims, but I smell the reek of deceit in the room."

Ris sniffed her armpit. "Hey, no stink here. Even after a night with the po-po, I think that's a bonus."

"Deceit." Harry squawked and flew at Patty. She nabbed him out of the air. The raven immediately stiffened into taxidermy.

"Wow. Nifty trick." Patty held the bird by his feet, upside down, and shook him.

"Leave my cursed Viking alone." Holly lurched forward and grabbed the girl's wrist. Her head dropped back and her eyes silvered. She turned, still holding Patty's wrist, and faced both girls. Images raced through her head of tall, muscular women with dark air and deep pits of black for eyes. Mocking laughter overlaid the vision and shadows crawled in and around the women. The phrase, *death, chaos, and discord* kept repeating in her head. Holly's connection broke when Patty yanked her wrist away and shoved the taxidermy Harry at Holly. Normal vision slowly filtered back, and Holly took a few deep, cleansing breaths.

The door to the bakery kitchen swung open, and a blonde woman in a pink power suit, chomping on a brownie, strolled in. She froze with the brownie halfway to her mouth as everyone stared. "What? I didn't think anyone would be here so early. I'll just..." She backed up.

"Marie Hestis." Lila pointed and growled. "Get your Keres nails off my brownies."

"But they're so good," Marie grumbled.

"I thought you were done when you collected the janitor. Why are you still here?" Holly forced her weird vision from her head and focused on the new Keres daimon.

"Well, I did have to pick up Leon. Then I got hangry and thought of the bakery." The daimon shrugged.

"See? Hangry. It drives you to do things." Colin

popped his head out from underneath the table. "Meanwhile, I could totally go for a second breakfast."

Rebus nodded at the daimon.

Marie coughed and thumped her chest. "You know, with all the people not dying, maybe it's a good idea if I hang around. It *is* Point Muse. There'll probably be another murder or two soon."

"The dead aren't dying?" Rebus looked concerned. "I need to call your mother. That's not normal. It shouldn't be happening."

The girls paled and Nate shuffled his feet, looking momentarily uncomfortable.

"Tell Mom it wasn't our fault." Patty chewed on the end of a black braid. She stepped away from the bakery door when a group of people entered, freezing for a moment as a customer pushed past her.

Holly frowned at the girl's reaction. Neither girl had seemed nervous until the group of customers had entered. What had changed?

Ris nodded, backing up next to her sister. "Nothing to do with us." She exchanged a loaded glance with her sister before continuing, "But we're pretty sure we know who was responsible. We can identify them, but we need... We want..." She trailed off and Patty broke in.

"Amnesty. We want amnesty from prosecution... And torture by parents." She crossed her arms and wrinkled her nose at her father. "Do we have a deal?"

Their father grabbed their arms, and misty shadows tangled around their wrists. "We will talk about this and your actions back at the inn." He spied Nate, rubbing the back of his head. "There's obviously something wrong with both you and Point Muse. Don't worry, we'll get to the bottom of it soon, son." He dragged the girls to the door but paused and spoke over his shoulder. "In case you don't remember, your name is Nate Mortis, and you have a very large family, with interfering parents and way too many siblings, including these two miscreants. We'll talk later."

Nate took a few steps forward and then watched the trio leave. He stretched his neck before rubbing at his head.

Holly planted herself in front of him. "You have family. Explains the squabbling with those two women."

"Supposedly." He grimaced. "And before you ask, I don't have any memories back. But I'm having flashes. Images. And they're in them." He nodded at the departed trio as they argued along Main Street. He made a face. "Mostly causing chaos."

"You look constipated." Harry hopped onto the table. "You need an Elspeth special. Bowel issues can be serious." He bobbed his head. "Not enough fiber in jail food. Maybe it's contagious? Stay away from the banshee, just in case."

A figure peeled away from the group of customers that had headed for the counter. *Samuel Wood.*

Smoothing his bottle-green, frock coat he sneered at Holly. "Spending your time wisely, I see. Nights at the police station, then lounging at the bakery. Your work ethic is disappointing. Your future replacement won't have the same issue." He sniffed as if he'd smelled a foul odor.

That's it. She couldn't stand the bakery or the people in it any longer. Holly let out a toned-down banshee shriek and clenched her fists.

"*Fight. Fight,*" Elspeth chanted and clapped her hands. "I just love the scent of blood and drama in the air. It's so invigorating, don't you think?"

"Nope. You can keep your invigorating blood to yourself. I just want peace and quiet." Holly ignored everyone in the bakery and stomped out onto Main Street. She closed her eyes and lifted her face to the weak morning sun and inhaled, letting all her worries drift away. The dead bodies, her firing,

Nate's almost burial, even her weird visions lately when she looked at Nate's sisters. The banshee pushed everything out of her mind and just breathed in and out.

"Is it always a madhouse in Point Muse, or was that a stupid question?" Nate moved to stand next to Holly on the sidewalk.

She cracked one eye open. "Stupid question and you're harshing my buzz."

"Buzz?"

"Meditation. Trying to rid my mind of annoyances."

"Is it working?"

"Not really." Giving in, the banshee cracked both eyes open. "We probably need to visit Mayweather Inn so you can speak with your family. See if your memories come back. Not to mention questioning Ris and Patty on who the killer is."

A black car with tinted windows accelerated along Main Street, catching her attention. The same car that forced her moped off the road near the Library... *The same car barreling toward them.*

"I get the feeling it's better to avoid the chaos."

"Watch out," Holly screeched, her skin itching madly as she looped an arm around Nate and threw her weight to the side. The black-colored car swerved, mounting the sidewalk and sending the duo to the ground as it sped off.

Nate curled his body around Holly and tried to cushion their fall.

The breath left Holly's body with a whomp and a wheeze as she hit the ground with Nate splayed under her. With a solid thump, Holly's head hit Nate's chest and she let herself slump over him.

The bakery door opened, and Elspeth stared down at the prostrate couple on the ground while munching on a lemon slice. "Banshee got dating game. Not even I would do that in public. *Kudos.*" Elspeth stepped over the couple and meandered along Main Street, whistling.

"I hate my family."

SEVENTEEN

"Have I mentioned how much I hate hospitals?" Holly whined as she shuffled into a better position on the bed in the curtained-off treatment room in Emergency.

"I concur. Too many plagues floating around in the air and the cesspool of germs." Harry's wings fluttered wildly until the pretty young nurse sashayed into the cubicle, then his wing drooped, and he hissed in pain.

"Oh, poor widdle birdie." The nurse placed a bright bandage on the raven's drooping wing and kissed his head. "That will fix you right up. You're too cute to be injured." The nurse turned to Holly with a smile. "He's such a cutie and so brave. Only bruises and scrapes, Ms. Harrow. Feel free to go. Mr. Mortis was lucky to escape with no injuries at all." She handed Holly a bunch of papers. "Just hand this to reception on the way out. And try to avoid speeding cars in the future." She blew Harry a kiss as she left the room.

Nate poked Harry's bandaged wing. "You were in the bakery when the car tried to run us over. You're not injured, you're just a big, feathered liar."

Harry sniffed. "I could've been hurt if I was outside with you. I'm widdle...er, little. I get hurt easily."

"You're a cursed Viking in the body of a sometimes taxidermied raven. You would have been fine. I think you have a thing for pretty nurses."

"You don't know what you're talking about, Fake Amnesia Boy." Harry clucked his beak, narrowly missing Nate's fingers.

"As fun as your squabbling can be, I need to get out of here before the police chief wants a statement. I suggest we skedaddle...*pronto*." Holly hopped down from the bed and winced as her feet hit the ground. She was achy from her impromptu flight to the ground, and as per usual, Nate had avoided any sort of injury. *Typical.* Tightening a grip on her papers, Holly headed back out to Emergency reception and handed the papers over. "Can you tell me how

Callista Demos is doing? She was admitted the other day after an accident."

A no-nonsense nurse eyed the disheveled banshee over the rim of her fire-engine red glasses. "Are you next of kin?"

"No. Part of the investigating team." Holly smiled ruefully and gestured to her ripped clothing and bruises. "As you can see, the investigation is ongoing."

Grunting, the nurse tapped the keyboard a few times. "She's still in a coma, but she is due for a doctor visit in an hour. We'll see how she responds then."

Holly nodded her thanks and waved to Nate to follow her.

"You want to check on Callista?" Nate matched his pace to Holly's, Harry flapping behind them.

"I just have a bad feeling, that's all. So many people dying, not dying..." Holly shrugged. "Something doesn't feel right."

"It's the hospital. It needs to be fumigated. A cesspool of germs. I told you that. *Cesspool.*" The raven said the word again with relish.

"Hospitals play an important part in human life. They provide healing when needed and support during and after traumatic events."

"Sounds like you're talking from experience or an

information pamphlet." It was starting to sound like Nate remembered more than he'd said. But why wouldn't he admit it?

"I have no clue." Nate rubbed the back of his head. "I'm just getting flashes."

"And your family?"

"Same thing. Images with no context. Flashes of faces, but that's all."

"That's probably enough of a confirmation. We can visit the inn after the hospital and speak to your dad." Holly grimaced. "On the other hand, I'd avoid those sisters of yours. They act way too much like Elspeth for my liking."

"Chaos lovers." Harry pretended to spit as he landed on Holly's shoulder. "Chaos and discord in their blood."

Sidestepping the people lining the hallway, Holly grimaced. "It's still busy here. I thought the dead alive thing had slowed down. Looks like no Death has made a big impact."

"Everyone tries to avoid Death. He's unwanted." Nate's face rippled, sadness gripping his features for a moment.

"Yeah, but he's needed. I mean...look around." Holly waved a hand at the people crowding the hallway still.

"People, human or supernatural, need closure, and death provides that. And why are you referring to death as a he? Could it be a she?"

Holly reached Callista's partially open hospital room door, and Harry lifted off the banshee's shoulder.

"No way I'm visiting a hospital room. Think of all the germs the people in this room have had." The raven shuddered and flapped back in the direction of the nurse's station.

Holly peeked into the room and surprised a capped, masked figure leaning over Callista, pillow in hand. "Oi," Holly screeched. The figure dropped the pillow, running straight at the banshee. The door flung open, and the masked figure slammed past Holly, knocking her to the ground before bolting.

Cursing, Nate crouched down next to Holly. "Are you okay?"

A familiar itch scratched the back of her neck and Holly lifted unseeing eyes to her sleuthing partner. Shadowed visions of a darkened underworld, voices screaming, moans loud in her ears, assaulted the banshee. An image of Leon stumbled into view, following a caped figure, both scrabbling through the uneven terrain, dodging grasping hands. A flash of light hair under the cape glowed.

Two oversized figures stood in the shadows, dark eyes gleaming, holding a shimmering door open. The hooded figure reached the door first and flung himself through, Leon following close behind. The oversized figures closed the door, spinning away into black shadows. Holly blinked rapidly as her vision dissipated. But a feeling of familiarity nagged at her. She knew Leon, but the caped figure and the shadowy giant figures struck a chord with her.

"Holly? You okay?" Concern lined Nate's features as he held out his hand.

Grasping at the hand, Holly pulled herself up. She shook her head to push the last of the vision away. "What are you doing? Ignore me. Get after that masked killer." She pushed Nate ahead of her as he took the hint, taking off running. Holly followed behind at a panting jog. She passed the nurse's station and yelled, "Someone just tried to suffocate Callista Demos. You need to check on her and call Chief Braun."

Harry zoomed up to Holly. "Are you running from the plague? Because I can tell you, that doesn't work."

"Someone tried to kill Callista. Nate's chasing the person and I'm chasing him."

"Never leave an amnesiac to do a Viking raven's

job." Harry poured on the flapping speed and pulled ahead of Nate, who sped up to match the bird. A contest of wills ensued. The warring duo disappeared behind a corner, and Holly groaned. "I am not built for cardio. None of the Harrows are." She pulled up at a still swinging door marked basement parking. "Why is it always a basement they run to?" Rubbing her heaving chest, Holly took the descending stairs carefully. The last thing she needed was to end up as a patient in the hospital again instead of just a visitor. At the bottom of the stairs, in front of an exit door, Nate and Harry argued.

"Why should a defenseless bird be the first in? Is this some sort of taxidermy prejudice?" Harry flapped his wings and protested.

The muscles along Nate's jaw twitched. "I am not prejudiced. It's logical. You can't die. You're a cursed Viking."

"Why are you arguing?" Holly staggered to a stop and leaned against the wall. "I'm never eating Lila's baked goods again. They murder my aerodynamics."

"Coffin Boy wants to use me as cannon fodder."

"Because you can't die," Nate burst out.

Holly rolled her eyes. "This is a ridiculous discussion. I'll go first."

"No."

"No way."

Nate put out an arm, barring Holly's way. "You've had enough accidents today. I don't want you anywhere near a dark underground parking level." Nate eased the exit door open. "Viking up, bird."

"Fine, but when I die a horrible death, I want a traditional burial. Grave gifts, funeral offerings, set on fire by blazing arrows. Standard stuff."

Nate grabbed hold of the raven and pitched him through the door. "Feel free to go Viking on the killers. Yell when it's all clear." He slammed the door shut and pressed his lips together, but Holly could still see the faint smile that twitched the corners of his lips.

"You enjoyed that," Holly accused.

"I've no idea what you're talking about." Nate crossed his arms. "I'm just making sure we use our best resources while we hunt the killer."

"But you still enjoyed throwing Harry into the parking garage."

An impish grin quirked one side of Nate's mouth, and his hazel eyes twinkled.

Holly fought the urge to drool. She averted her eyes. "Can you hear anything yet?"

They both paused to listen as a large bang sounded, followed by the squeal of spinning tires.

"That's it. I'm done waiting." Rushing past Nate, Holly sped into the parking garage. Flickering neon lights partially lit the garage. "Harry? Are you okay? Can you hear me?" Pausing her frantic rushing, Holly listened for any sign of her cursed Viking familiar.

Multiple thumps and unintelligible murmurings sounded from a trashcan shoved behind a concrete pillar. Heading for the noise, Holly gingerly grabbed the lid and lifted it, exposing a garbage-covered, beady-eyed raven with a drooping, black banana skin hanging over his face.

"You. Will. Fumigate. Me." Harry snapped his beak at the hanging banana skin.

Pursing her lips together, Holly carefully picked up the banana skin without bursting out into gales of laughter. "What happened?"

"I lost the figure between the cars. Next thing I knew, I got hit with the trash can lid and buried in this dented, smelly metal coffin."

Reaching in, Holly extracted Harry and held him at arm's length. "I owe you. And I promise a pamper session with Mom's potions and lotions. But first, you need a bath. *Bad.*" She pushed the raven at

Nate. "Hold him. It's your penance for sacrificing him."

Nate spluttered, then grudgingly took the bird. Despite his disgruntled expression, he cradled Harry against his chest.

"We need to head back to Callista. See if she's okay." Returning to the stairwell, Holly sighed as she eyed the climb. "I really hate exercise." Putting her head down, she powered up the stairs and into the hallway before heading back to the nurse's station. Catching her breath, Holly leaned against the counter. "Is Callista Demos okay?"

The nurse grimaced and shook her head. "I'm sorry. There was nothing we could do. We notified Chief Braun, and his deputies are already on site. Her room's a crime scene now."

"Did she..." Holly trailed off, unsure how to broach the coming back to life issue.

"We waited for the required amount of time for reanimation, but she didn't. The patient's one of our very few true dead. She's been moved to the morgue for further review." The nurse pointed at a younger looking doctor with a shock of red hair chatting up a harried looking nurse. "Dr Targa is scheduled for the morgue. He might be able to help with information."

Holly thanked the nurse and turned away.

"I'm sorry. But if she was killed, she won't be coming back. Non-violent deaths only," Nate reminded her.

"I know. I was just hoping for good news for once."

"Good news is only bad news waiting to happen." Harry poked a wing at Nate. "Watch how you carry me, you overgrown behemoth. I'm a fragile raven."

Ignoring them, Holly headed for the doctor. "Dr Targa. A moment of your time?"

The redheaded doctor turned, and the nurse used the distraction to escape. Sporting a wry smile, the doctor greeted them. "Ah, the town's banshee, a cursed Viking, and an amnesiac stranger."

Holly's eyes rounded. "Are you psychic?" she blurted out.

The doctor let out a gale of laughter. "I wish. No. I just listen to gossip. It's a flaw I wholly embrace. What can I do for you?"

"Callista Demos, the coma patient who just passed away. Have you had had a chance to look at her?"

"Not yet. I've only had a cursory examination. Then again, it's not like I'm currently overwhelmed with patients. I should get through the examination relatively quickly."

"In your cursory glance, did you see anything noteworthy?" Holly pushed.

"You're not law enforcement officially but you *are* a Harrow. I'm happy to give you an off the record opinion."

"Thanks, Doc. I appreciate it."

Harry and Nate kept quiet next to Holly, letting her take the lead.

"Cursory examination showed some petechial hemorrhaging in the eyes. It's likely she was suffocated somehow."

"Would a pillow over the face do it?"

"That would fit. Now, if you excuse me, I'll get back to work." He nodded goodbye to the trio.

Holly blew out a breath. "Definitely murder."

Someone was removing loose ends. And Nate's sisters had just announced in the bakery this morning that they knew who the killer was...

EIGHTEEN

"About time you turned up." Rose Mayweather glared at Holly, Nate, and Harry. Her silver bouffant hairdo had stray pieces of hair sticking out everywhere. And her nineteen fifties style blue dress, with lime-green petticoats underneath, hung lopsided, and the inn owner's cheeks were flame red.

"Since when do you welcome Harrows and Harry? You can't stand any of us." The back of Holly's neck itched and not in an impending vision kind of way. More like an Elspeth-caused, impending doom feeling. "What has she done now?"

"Who?" Nate appeared confused.

Harry rolled his beady eyes and snapped at the clueless man still holding him. "Elspeth, of course. It's always the wicked witch." The raven shook himself and pushed against Nate's arms, lifted into the air, and hopped onto Holly's shoulder, still holding his wing with the bandage at a weird angle.

"What's wrong with the bird?" Rose eyed Harry's wing before she wrenched her gaze away. The inn owner couldn't stand the mouthy bird and freaked out every time he turned taxidermy. Harry being Harry lived to torment her with it.

"I, the brave Viking, sacrificed myself to hunt a killer. Because that's just what warrior heroes do."

"You were thrown into a trash can, and I had a fish you out."

"But I did it heroically."

"I don't care." Rose tapped a red-painted nail on her reception counter. "You need to deal with that wicked grandmother of yours. I can't have her threatening paying guests. I have to draw a line."

"Speaking of guests, do you have a Rebus Mortis booked in? Or a Ris and Patty Mortis?" Nate worked his jaw as he stared at Rose, purposefully not looking at Holly as he asked.

Rose narrowed her eyes. "We have a policy of not giving out room numbers. Privacy issues and all that."

"We're family. He's my father."

Oh yeah. Nate was definitely hiding something.

His words made it sound like he remembered his family perfectly. Why hide it?

"Uh huh." Rose made a noncommittal noise and pointed to the dining room. "Mr. Mortis is currently having a snack in the dining room with his daughters if you wish to join them."

Nate glanced at Holly and raised an eyebrow in a silent question.

"Go do the family thing. It will help your *memory*." Holly stressed the last word. "Find your sisters. I'll deal with Elspeth." She waved him off and turned to Rose. "All right. Lay the calamity on me. What has she done?"

Rose pointed at the bar. "I have no words to describe it. Just deal with it." She pursed her lips tight, refusing to say another word.

"Alrighty then. Once more into an Elspeth-caused breach." Holly mentally girded her loins for battle and flung the door open to chaos. Black, shadowy cobweb tendrils stretched from corner to corner of the room, crisscrossing the bar except for a puddle of light focused on Elspeth's pug minion. He didn't seem discombobulated at all by the shadow cobwebs hanging over the room and instead, continued licking his nether regions. "Could you not do that in public, Colin?"

"Dog's gotta do what a dog's gotta do when he's gotta do it." Colin stopped his bathing and shook himself. "These dames got issues. It's a dominance fight. They both want to be top dog. Good luck." The pug settled down and closed his eyes, proceeding to let out dainty little snores.

"Wish I could have a nap," Holly muttered, then raised her voice. "Cut the dark hag act, Elspeth. You're freaking Rose out, to the point she actually welcomed me to Mayweather Inn."

Amber eyes popped up in the far corner and blinked. "Why is it always my fault? Ever thought someone else might be involved?"

"Nope. It's always you." Holly raised her hand and struck off each finger as she spoke. "Mouthy, snarky, attitude, chaos-lover." She held up a closed fist. "See? No fingers. Now cut the shadows off, or I'll tell Lila and Xandie to ban you from corrupting any future offspring."

"Offspring?" Elspeth's corner lightened. "I'm the best. Kids love me. Future spawn will follow me around, wanting to be just like me."

"Future offspring. *Future*," Holly stressed. "And not if you don't get rid of the shadow gunk."

"Bartering away the state of the souls of one's future great-grandchildren is truly an Elspeth thing to do." A rich, warm, dark voice flowed from the opposite corner to Elspeth.

Holly flashed back to her original vision when she'd touched the silver chains binding Nate. Warm shadows, the welcoming flap of wings. She forced the vision away and focused on the task at hand. "Right. I don't care who started it or why you're fighting in the bar. Draw your inner hags back and get rid of the freaky shadow webs now. Otherwise, I'll send Rose in, and she can nag you both until you scream your surrender. "

Amber eyes blinked furiously. "I can't stand that woman's whining. Her voice sets my wigs on edge." The wicked witch of Point Muse snapped her fingers and the shadows receded, writhing, and rolling like snakes hopped up on sugar. Colin stopped snoring and shuddered as black tendrils trailed over his fur, leaving it standing on end.

"Man, my queen. You know I hate it when you do that." The pug shook himself and meandered over to the bar before collapsing against it.

Holly spun and pointed to the opposite corner where more dark, warm shadows gathered. "You, too, whoever you are, or I send in the nuclear option. I'm sure someone's fed the dog seafood today. Trust me, you do not want to try him." Holly jerked her head at the again slumbering pug. Colin loved food... All food. But seafood didn't agree with him and caused an upset stomach and vile, virulent, and radioactive flatulence. Elspeth's minion was the wicked witch's go-to secret weapon for taking down enemies. A sweep of air sliced against her cheek and Holly winced as Harry's talons gripped her shoulder tight. "I thought you'd deserted me for Rose?"

"Never fear, banshee. The inn owner is no fun to torment when she's already worked up over Elspeth." Harry settled comfortably against Holly's neck. "Have the hags bowed to my banshee's magnificence? Or have they expired from a shadow-born plague?"

"We have one hold out." Holly cocked her shiny, brown bob, and it swung smoothly around her chin. "Well? Dial it back or I send in the pug along with a hypochondriac, cursed Viking raven, and he can send you into a declining depression as he regales you with a list of his many, many ailments."

"I can't help it if I have a delicate constitution." The raven sniffed.

"You're stuffed." Holly pointed out fairly. "You shouldn't have a list of ailments."

"You'll be stuffed if you keep hanging with that so-called amnesiac. Who knows what germs rampage in that man's body since being chained in a coffin."

"I do have a sore throat," the banshee admitted and tried to swallow through the lump.

The raven flapped a wing and slapped it against her forehead. "You're hot. Maybe we should quarantine you?"

A low mumbling of warm laughter danced across Holly's senses as the shadows turned into tiny blackbirds, revealing a small curvy woman with long black, curly hair with silver streaks, dark eyes, and pale skin. The blackbirds enclosed the woman in dark clothing with tiny twinkling silver stars. "My little Nate, spending time with a hypochondriac bird and banshee. What a shakeup. I knew forcing him to have a vacation was the right idea." The woman frowned for a moment. "What's this about a coffin and a chain?"

Holly gripped the bridge of her nose. Maybe she needed another holiday away from Point Muse. Somewhere with a beach and sugary, alcoholic drinks with little umbrellas. "We found Nate chained by a Hephaestus-forged metal in a coffin. He'd been hit on the head. We're trying to chase down his would-be killer and help him get his memory back. I take it you're his mother? I've met his father and sisters already."

The woman clapped her hands, and black sparks

shot out in every direction. "I'm Nyxie. I heard my little boy had an accident on his vacation but a coffin?"

"Someone knocked him out. I was supposed to bury the coffin he was hidden in, but I found him first. Chained tight. When I touched it, it fell off. But now people are dying." Holly nibbled the edge of her lip. "Well, some people are. The murdered ones. Everyone else is staying alive. And the killer's trying to hurt us too. Multiple accidents." Holly waved a hand, dismissing her words. "The question is why are you throwing down with Elspeth in the Mayweather Inn bar?"

"Ask Nyxie pooh-pooh," Elspeth sneered and hauled herself up onto a barstool.

"None of this is my fault, Elly. I just wanted my baby boy to have a vacation. Meet someone. How could I know some psycho would target him and involve your Harrow banshee?" The tiny woman crossed her arms and glared at Elspeth's bright yellow, braided wig. "And that's not your color. You should stick to blues and brown."

"Elly?" Holly shuddered. Cutesy nicknames gave her digestion. Especially when in connection to Elspeth.

"I've known Elspeth Harrow for a very long time.

She's equal parts delight and horror. Just how I like my besties."

Nyxie blew a kiss at the glaring witch.

"Bestie is stretching it. The last time I saw Nyxie, she left me in Hades' vault and double-crossed me."

"But sweetie, Shade released you, and I got a lovely, cursed pair of earrings. Win-win."

Elspeth tapped her orange-painted nails on the bar countertop. "We sometimes have aligning objectives and temporarily ally ourselves," she hissed at the other woman.

"And here we are, vacationing in Point Muse together."

"I owe my son-in-law a favor, and you know how I feel about that."

Her grandmother hated owing anyone with a burning passion. And Elspeth burning with anything was *not* a good idea. "Can we shelve the warring egos for a moment? We have bigger fish to fry, and we need to find Nate's sisters as well. They could be in trouble."

"Good luck. Nyxie has a mind of her own and it's rarely on target." Nate's father stood in the bar's doorway, Nate hovering behind.

"Rebus," Nyxie complained. "You're a meanie."

Nate stepped around his father and focused on Holly. "You're okay? Mom can be overwhelming to the uninitiated."

"I live with Elspeth. I think I can cope." Holly faced Nate, arms crossed. "I take it your memory has miraculously healed itself."

Nate rubbed the back of his neck. "Not completely. But more and more bits are sliding into place, and I'm definitely related to them. They forced me on vacation here in Point Muse."

"Uh huh." Holly raised an interrogative eyebrow.

"Deceit." Harry snapped his beak and lifted into the air, diving at Nate. "Deceiver. A Viking warrior would never let you near his volva after all your lies. Lost memory, bah."

"My memory isn't completely back, and I didn't want to raise any hopes. Then I saw Ris, Patty, and my father and recognized them."

"Don't blame our baby boy." Nyxie strolled over and wrapped her arm around her son. "I booked Nate into the inn and let the girls arrange everything else. They were supposed to organize transport and activities. We have no idea how we ended up with him in a coffin."

"That's why we're here. Pretty sure your girls know what happened. We need to speak to them.

We think they know who hurt Nate and killed the other people."

Nyxie snorted. "Good luck. Those two only have chaos, cakes, and chocolate on their minds."

"The girls headed back to their room. I'm sure they'll be happy to talk to you. In fact, we all have some questions." Rebus' hazel eyes hardened. "If they know what's good for them."

Ignoring everyone, Holly stomped out into reception and stopped in front of Rose's desk. The banshee slapped the counter. "Patty and Ris Mortis' room number."

"Room seven," Rose offered without a fight, eyes wide.

Holly stomped up the stairs, Harry fluttering behind her. Reaching the room, the banshee thumped on the door. Not waiting for an answer, she shoved the door open...*into chaos.*

A clothing tsunami had washed over the room, covering every available surface, including the twin beds, in colorful material. The twin bed mattresses lay half on, half off their bases and a small chair rested on its side.

"The girls are messy, but not this bad." Rebus and Nyxie, along with Nate and Elspeth, crowded into the room.

Holly took a step to the side and stumbled over something heavy underfoot. Wincing, Holly bent over and picked up the offending object. It was a heavy metal link. Holly straightened and held out the metal to Elspeth. "Recognize this?" A heavy silver link of metal sat on Holly's hand.

"How the Hecate did that get here?" Elspeth poked the link. "It was stolen from my lair, so why's it here?"

"I think it was used on Nate's sisters. I think the killer has them."

A black mass filled the hallway, pressing into the room, but this time it wasn't welcoming. Shadows formed edges, slicing the air like wings...crow wings this time. A strident cawing filled Holly's ears with mocking laughter, promising retribution. Claws sliced through the banshee's hair, Harry flapped on Holly's shoulder, trying to encircle her with his wings. Trying to protect.

"Right. Everyone, calm down. We can formulate a non-crazy, free of Harrow mayhem plan to get the girls back." Nate's voice carried over the sound of the shadow crows flapping their wings. "Yeah. Something you should know. No one crosses my family and some of us have anger issues..."

Sounds like they're related to Elspeth...

NINETEEN

"And my shadows can suck the life out of you." Elspeth jutted her jaw out, amber eyes aflame with competition.

"Well, my shadows can tie you into knots and stick you against the wall."

The wicked witch patted the lounge room wall in Harrow house. "And my house can disappear, so you'll never be found again. What do you think of that, Nixie pooh-poohed?"

"I think..."

Holly tuned out the squabbling hags and glanced around the room. After finding Nate's sisters missing, Holly had called a family war council. Everyone returned to Harrow House to formulate a plan of attack. *If they weren't so busy arguing.*

"It'll be fine. They're just letting off steam." Matthew Grimm, Lila's boyfriend, ran a hand down Lila's hellhound Nash's slumbering back.

"How did your trip to see your parents go? Did you find anything out about people not dying?" Matthew's entire family were reapers and collected souls for Thanatos, Death personified. The Grimm family had placed Matthew permanently in Point Muse since the town's death toll tended to fluctuate more than normal.

"The underworld's still maintaining Thanatos is too busy to see anyone, but Mom has a friend who works in his office. He hasn't been in for days. Apparently, something big's happening and he has to sort it out in person."

"Why something big? Can't it be something little that's easy to fix?" Holly grouched.

Matthew smiled and flicked the banshee on the nose. "It's the Harrow bad luck. What can go wrong, will go wrong." He slid Nash off his lap and onto the couch he and Holly perched on. "I might rescue Nate from your mom and his dad. I think they were discussing recipes and Nate's eyes glazed over." The tall, muscled reaper strolled over to the trio, quickly extracting Nate. They disappeared out into the hallway.

"Wonder what that's about."

Xandie paused in cuddling her new husband. "What's what about?" She reached for a slice of pizza and took a large bite, mumbling around a full mouth. "Geez, these pizzas Aunt Winifred made are yummy."

"Can't say doll face is wrong. My Winnie has a gift with food." Colin, the mouthy pug, waddled across to the girls with a large, zippered pack strapped around his chest.

"Do I want to know why you're carrying a pug bag around?"

"You make fun of me, banshee. But Colin will save the day. This is my rescue snack pack. Full of energy food to help my secret weapon."

Holly rolled her eyes. "I want to know but I kinda don't."

"Well, sweet cheeks. It's a rescue, which means there's a villain, so I need to be able to roll my weapon out at any stage." Colin patted his snack bag. "Tuna crackers. I eat them. You point me in the direction of our victim, and I let loose."

Shuddering, Holly moved as far away on the couch as she could get from the radioactive pug. Colin loved all food, but seafood didn't love him back. In fact, it disagreed with his stomach so much, it mutated into radioactive flatulence Elspeth called her olfactory weapon of mass destruction. "Don't explode around me. We still need to plan a rescue attempt."

Lila placed another plate of hot mini pizzas on the coffee table in front of everyone. "There's no seafood in these and no pineapple either." Lila pretended to gag. "Only psychos like pineapple on pizza."

"The whole of the family should love pineapple pizza then." Zach snagged a few pizzas and shoved them in. "Only thing I like better is honey. Lots of honey."

"Thank Hecate you're not in charge of food. You'd need to see the dentist weekly...or the dietician." Holly poked fun at the bear shifter.

"Toothache is no joke. It can fell the strongest warrior." Harry dipped overhead until he alighted on the back of the couch.

"I need to grab Nate and Matthew. Get our planning on." Holly nodded.

"Things will be much clearer with a plan. A plan is exactly what we need. A true warrior always has a plan and a back-up." Harry bobbed up and down.

"Get the feeling the banshee and the raven want

to plan?" Xandie poked her husband in the ribs and giggled.

He shot her a pointed glance. "Sometimes a plan is a good idea, instead of running in like a Harrow, riding on the buzz of chaos and mayhem and not knowing what to do."

"Buzz kill," Xandie accused her husband.

"I'm ignoring all of you." Holly gripped the bridge of her nose. They all made fun of her need for a plan but considering the chaos and mayhem that interfered daily in a Harrow life, any extra help was a good thing.

Holly paused at the living room entrance to the hallway and popped her head out. The two men stood at one end, speaking quietly, heads together. Matthew tried to hand his grim reaper staff to Nate, who shook his head and handed it back. The reaper bowed his head and took a step back. *What the?* Lila's boyfriend was acting like Nate was the king of Harrow House, not plain old Amnesiac Boy. What else wasn't he telling her?

A banging on the front door surprised a squeal out of Holly and both men spun. She held up a hand. "I'll get it." She rushed to the heavy wooden door and opened it, surprising Dolly, the troll receptionist from the funeral home. "What's up, Dolly? You okay?" It was never good when funeral home business came calling at your house.

Clad in a baby-blue business suit, the towering troll receptionist looked over her square shoulder. Her cheeks paled as she nervously patted her bristly, dark hair. "I know Mr. Woods fired you, and you're no longer an employee, at least until our normal bosses are back from their family leave, but I need to talk to you."

Holly opened the door wider. "You're welcome to come in, if you want."

Dolly shifted in her matching blue-suede pumps that resembled large boats. "I don't want anyone seeing me here." She took a shallow breath and a muscle worked in her jaw. "Mr. Wood has been acting weird. Carrying boxes to his car, shutting himself in his office and..." Dolly paused dramatically before continuing, "He gave us all a two-day vacation. Middle of the week? Who does that?"

"That's not Samuel. He's never nice. And he would never interrupt a working week." *A vacation?* Holly would have thought he'd set himself alight before making friendly overtures to the employees. What was he planning?

Dolly lowered her voice. "I stayed back to empty your locker. Sorry, but he made me."

Shrugging, Holly motioned for the troll to continue.

"I boxed your stuff and went to drop it in the loading bay and saw a black SUV parked, with a stranger standing beside the car."

"Did you see his face?"

"No. Whoever it was wore this weird, hooded cape that covered their face. All I could tell is that they were short. But I heard muffled voices yelling. Females, I think? But I couldn't see anything else. Samuel sprung me."

"Are you okay? I mean after Samuel sprung you?" Dolly needed to lay low in case Samuel saw the troll as a threat.

"He demanded to know what I was doing. I showed him your box and told him I was dropping it off in the loading area. But he yanked the door closed and said he was busy. He told me not to show up for work until notified, otherwise I'd be fired as well." She looked shamefaced. "I just scooted out. I'm not exactly the bravest of trolls."

Holly leaned forward and gave their receptionist a quick hug. "You did the right thing. Something's wrong with Samuel and we'll find out exactly what he's hiding. You need to do what he said. Find someplace to lay low. Somewhere protected."

"I'll head home to Mom and Dad; no one's going to take on an entire clan of trolls. But I could go back to spy if you need me to."

A thousand ants inched along Holly's arm and an image wavered in her vision. Dolly's solid form now had holes poked through it. Her eyes stared unseeing back at Holly for a moment. The banshee closed her eyes tight and swallowed around a large lump in her throat a few times. "No. It's safer if you don't go back to the funeral home until Samuel's gone." Holly opened her eyes to a thankfully solid and concerned Dolly. Holly forced a smile. "Banshee thing. Don't worry. Just head home. Stay with your family until I call you. Okay?"

Dolly nodded and shoved the box of Holly's things at her. She gave a wave as the troll headed back to her tank-sized car.

Juggling the box on her hip, Holly slammed the door shut and exhaled. Samuel had made his move and had Nate's sisters at the funeral home. The question was why? Why would a fill-in funeral director want to kidnap two complete strangers... "Unless they aren't strangers?" Holly mused out loud.

"You okay?" Nate stood a few paces away and concern lined his features.

"Dolly just wanted to drop off this box with my

things and let me know Samuel was acting weird at the funeral home. She thinks she heard muffled female voices yelling out from a black SUV that was parked in the loading docks."

Nate stiffened as his mother, Nyxie, appeared behind them. "You know where my sisters are?"

Holly nodded. "I do. And it's planning time. We've got two annoying girls to rescue."

***

"It's a solid plan. Why can't anyone follow it?" Nate crouched. "We all planned together. It was clear."

"Blame your mother and my grandmother. It's their fault. They're the ones who went rogue." Holly wrinkled her nose. "Frankly, I expected it. I don't know about your mother, but Elspeth isn't the most dependable Harrow out there. At least your dad's sticking to the plan. That's something."

"Winifred listened."

"Mom is used to Harrow rescue attempts. She'll make sure food and first-aid are ready. And Mom knows with Xandie and the police chief in the funeral home, and Grimm and some reapers friends patrolling outside, we'll be safe. I think she'd rather be back up at the house, anyway. By the way, we're gonna have to have a talk about you and the reapers soon." Holly shot Nate a sideways glance. "Got me?" When Matthew's reaper friends had turned up as back-up, the reaction to Nate had been the same pale faces and deep respect. Not something Harrows were used to. Holly was definitely missing something. At least for now. She had a sneaking suspicion she knew exactly what Nate was hiding.

Harry bobbed up and down on the gravestone that Nate and Holly were crouched behind. "Listen to my banshee. She speaks the truth."

Nate threaded his fingers with Holly's. "I promise you, when we get my sisters back, I will fill you in on everything."

Holly leaned against his hard shoulders and stared up into his hazel eyes, which she could barely make out because of the darkened night. "I take it you remember everything now?"

"A few patchy areas, mostly around the time of the head knock. But yes, I know who I am. Completely." Nate flicked Holly a concerned glance. "I'm just wondering if it will change how you see me."

"If you're a serial killer, I'm outta here. Possibly also if you're a doctor. They're around way too many germs." Holly snickered and then clapped a hand over her mouth and peered around the massive gravestone. She untangled their hands and patted Nate's arm. "Maybe we should shelve this bonding for later."

"My ears would welcome respite from your prattling." Harry spoke quietly over their heads. "And a return to our battle plan would be appreciated."

Holly tracked Samuel as he dragged two chain-bound women to an open area near a freshly dug grave. "I think they're bound with the same chain you were."

Nate crowded close, peering around Holly. "They're probably feeling drained. That's what it did to me. Are they okay?"

"Judging by the gestures and the muffled curses, I think they're fine. Except for the chain."

"What do we do with Samuel after we rescue my sisters?"

"Lila said her dad and Hades, God of the under-world, are dropping in and grabbing him. Taking him to Tartarus. Leon was one of Hades' escaped prisoners, but since he's dead, he's back in Tartarus already."

"And Samuel? Do you think he's the other escaped prisoner?"

Holly watched as Samuel poked the girls with a

shovel and taunted them. "I think Tartarus will be a perfect spot for him."

"But we saw someone search Callista's apartment in a hooded cape and you've had a vision of a killer in a cape. But there isn't one anywhere near him."

"He could have left it in the funeral home or his SUV or..." Holly trailed off. She was pretty sure she'd just worked out exactly what was happening.

"Or? Don't leave me hanging. Finish the sentence." Nate's voice hitched.

"I think I need to send Harry in to scout the area." She eyed her Viking raven. "You good to do aerial reconnaissance?"

"Good has many definitions. I am ready to leave this field of the dead. So, aerial viewing it is." The raven shook out his feathers and lifted into the air.

His claws glanced over Holly's head, ruffling her hair. A banshee wail clawed at the inside of her throat, demanding release. She tried to fight it back, but it was pointless. The wail echoed through the dark and silent graveyard. Samuel had already heard.

"Why don't you join us, banshee, since you've already announced your presence."

Panting, Holly levered herself upright and yelled, "Harry, get out of there." Her banshee wail had been triggered by the vision of Harry falling life-less—*permanently lifeless*—to the ground.

"Join me, Ms. Harrow. I'd love to educate you on the procedure of a correctly carried out live burial," Samuel mocked the banshee. "By the way, our John Doe might as well join us too. Saves me from having to hunt him down later. Snipping loose ends and all that."

Nate clambered to his feet, grabbed Holly's hand, and clasped it tight.

Holly gave him a quick squeeze back before dropping his hand. She moved to stand at the edge of an open grave. Nate's sisters were bound and gagged to the side, glaring at everyone.

Samuel poked the women with his shovel again, eliciting grunts.

Surging forward, Nate teetered on the edge of the grave, teeth bared, hair curling wildly around his head in a dark halo.

"Now, now Mr. Doe... Or is it Mortis? Or something else?" Samuel smirked, apparently enjoying the theatrics and threats. "I suggest you stand down. Death isn't in charge here... *Not anymore.*"

Holly's only warning was Nate's sisters' widening eyes before a voice spoke out from the dark of the night.

"He's right." Sissy Corey, in a black cape with the hood down, stood in the dim light of Samuel's lantern, her snow-white hair arranged in angelic curls around her head. Her pale blue eyes sparkled with energy, and in her hand...

A short, black, adamantine sickle.

"Death isn't in charge anymore. I am."

TWENTY

"Point Muse's own Mrs. Claus look-alike, with the personality of a piranha. I am so surprised," Holly intoned in a sarcastic voice, making sure she had a tight hold on the back of Nate's shirt. She'd seen him go still as soon as he spotted Sissy and the sickle. She'd bet her last Harrow dollar the final pieces of his missing memory just slotted back into place.

A surprisingly girly laugh sprang from Sissy. "I'll take that as a compliment, Ms. Harrow." Sissy pretended to scratch her head with the sickle before letting out another peel of hysterical laughter. Then she calmed down with the odd heaving giggle or two. "My, I haven't laughed like that in decades. Incarceration doesn't induce hilarity normally."

"You're one of Hades' escaped prisoners."

"I am *the* escaped prisoner. Leon was just a lucky tagalong. Benefiting from all my handiwork."

"Lucky until *you killed him*, you mean." Holly tightened her grip on Nate, trying to pull him back from the literal edge.

"Honestly, the temerity of some people." Sissy shook her head. "You think the fact that I allowed him his freedom, let him follow me here to Point Muse, would be enough. But no." Sissy used the sharp sickle to trim her nails, Nate's eyes followed her every motion. "He had to bring his mouthy girlfriend."

"And Arnold Twigg?" Okay, he was a blackmailer and creepy, but he didn't deserve death by broomstick.

"Said mouthy girlfriend and Leon fought in public. Twigg overheard and put two and two together and came up with cash." Sissy tsked. "Really, people these days are so grasping and greedy."

"And your thickheaded lackey here?" Holly speared a glance at a nervous Samuel, who kept adjusting his Victorian top hat.

Samuel dropped his hands when he noticed the banshee watching. "I'm no lackey, banshee. I'm an integral part of the plan."

"Prison pen-pal." Sissy rolled her eyes.

"True love," Samuel corrected.

"Seriously? Stuck in the underworld for a crime and you get correspondence?"

"One of Hades' new measures to help rehabilitation." Sissy giggled. "It helped rehabilitate me right out of prison. That and a few allies, of course. I couldn't have done anything without them."

Holly reached up a second hand to grip the other side of Nate's shirt. If her guesses were correct, this wouldn't be pretty. "Do tell, psycho Mrs. Claus."

Pointing at the girls, Sissy snapped her fingers. Samuel scuttled over and untied the gags.

Both women worked their jaws and glared daggers and death at Sissy.

"Isn't that better? Now you can tell your brother just how helpful you've both been. How much you contributed to his downfall."

"You tricked us." Ris spat on the ground and struggled against the chains.

"We had no clue what she planned to do, Nate, we swear." Patty nodded in agreement.

"They're emotional idiots, despite their illustrious parentage. I spun them a story about Samuel and me being star-crossed lovers. How he'd helped me turn over a new leaf. If only I could see him, my murderous ways would be behind me forever." Sissy giggled again. "The girls helped me break out and held a portal open. We settled into Point Muse life, but I needed a cash start-up."

"You blackmailed them." Not hard to work out where all the money had come from.

"She blackmailed *us*, the Tartarus cursed she-devil," Ris burst out. "We had no choice but to help. If anyone else found out..." She trailed off and her sister picked up the story.

"We'd never hear the end of it. Grow up. Take on your responsibilities," Patty mimicked. "Mom decided big bro needed a vacation and picked Point Muse." Patty sighed. "Talk about bad luck. We thought we could visit before they arrived and sort this all out. But we never imagined you'd decide to take down Death himself."

Nate froze and glanced over his shoulder at Holly, who still held onto his shirt with both hands.

She rolled her eyes. "Really? Did you think I'm stupid, Thanatos?" Holly let go of Nate and flexed her hands, forcing blood back into them. "Initially, I had no idea, but little pointers kept popping up. People stopped dying, the way Matthew, who collected souls for Thanatos, treated you. You with gaps in your memory. It wasn't hard. I'm a banshee.

We herald death... *Remember?*" Holly smiled at the startled Nate. "Just because I have a few issues with germs doesn't make me an idiot."

A muscle worked in Nate's jaw. He took a step back from the freshly dug grave and turned to Holly. "My mother thinks I work too hard and loves to meddle. The more chaos the better. She booked the hotel and dumped the rest of the planning on my sisters, Ris and Patty."

"Eris and Apate, the goddesses of strife and discord. That's why things kept going wrong around them and why they love chaos."

Nate nodded. "It was just supposed to be a vacation. Then I found that man dying of a heart attack, so I bent to help, and Sisyphus jumped me. Once she had chained me, there was nothing I could do. My energy and my powers drained."

"And the memory loss?" Holly clenched her fists. She hadn't wanted to help in the beginning, but she had. Slippery Death had worked his way under her defenses.

"In the beginning, there were only flashes. I truly had no clue who I was or what had happened. Then..."

"Then you saw your idiot sisters?"

He sighed but agreed with Holly. "Then I saw

those two fluff heads trailing us, and a big chunk came back."

"Hey," Ris protested.

"We aren't fluff heads. Mom told you to stop calling us that," Patty spat out.

"After I saw them and Dad, I just wanted to get my sickle and cape back, then tell you the whole story."

"Not happening, Natey." Sissy stroked her cape with her free hand. "This cape stores dead souls, which could come in handy. But I hate the damn butterflies following me everywhere."

"The butterflies are a representation of life," Holly explained. "Use the sickle and cape and you're going to leave a trail of butterflies. What do you really want, Sisyphus?"

Samuel cleared his throat. "What we want, dearest. *We.*"

Sissy cackled, sounding just like Elspeth. "Oh, no, lover. It really is what *I* want. Your wishes have never mattered. You're a means to an end."

Holly pasted a sympathetic expression on her face. "Poor Samuel. You provided the link to Point Muse, to the funeral home, and a way to dispose of Nate's body and now, his sisters. That was it."

Nate drew himself up. "I'm willing to exchange myself for my sisters."

Holly blew a raspberry. "Let me educate you, Mister Hero. She doesn't want your sisters or even you. She's after bigger fish. She wants Hades."

Sissy whistled. "Banshee's smarter than a god. I'm impressed."

Backing away, Samuel shook his head wildly. "No. That wasn't the plan. This was about ransoming idiot goddesses and getting money for a new life together. Not taking on the god of the underworld. " He tripped over a headstone and collapsed on the ground, his top hat rolling a few paces away.

"That was your plan, not mine."

"But I loved you," Samuel wailed and hit the grass with a fist.

"Wow." Who knew Samuel Wood had a functioning heart? Holly shuffled a few steps off to the side, readying herself.

Raising Death's sickle, Sisyphus stepped up to the bound goddesses. She ran the sickle over the women's faces and carefully sliced a few strands of hair from each of them. "I really love this weapon. So light, so sharp." She smirked. "You know, it's amazing what one can find out these days. These Hephaestus-forged chains render a god or goddess mortal, then if you take their soul with Death's sickle? *Bam.* True death for a divine. And I will do it if you don't get Hades here right now."

"Seriously. This is all about Hades? It's such a letdown." Holly just needed to keep Sissy villain-monologuing for a little longer.

"Hades ruined my life. He entombed me in Tartarus for eternity. Over a few pesky murders, that's all. Just a few family members and a handful of paltry inn guests. And for that, I'm tormented eternally. It's not fair," Sissy bellowed into the dark night.

The spreading night seemed to be darker nearer Sissy the boasting killer than anywhere else. Holly sighed. So much for her plan. She hated it when people went rogue. Sticking to a plan was so much neater.

"Always such a drama queen, Sisyphus." Nate's mother's voice echoed out of the threatening shadows. Tendrils fluttered toward Sissy like the edges of crows' wings. A breeze blew through the graveyard, fluttering the bottom of Sisyphus' cape. The butterflies grouped around the cape's hem disappeared with a pop. Nyxie took a step out of the shadows, two crows in pride of place on her diminutive shoulders. Her long dark, gray-streaked hair streamed behind her, and her black dress glittered with shadows and stars.

Rebus stepped to his wife's side, tall and muscled. His curly, dark hair had silver streaks radiating from the temples. His eyes were deep pits made of darkness and he wore a matching suit of shadows. "Don't interrupt a villain's speech, dear. They're always so entertaining."

"Nyx, Goddess of the night, and Erebus, God of darkness." Sissy turned an incredulous gaze on Nate. "You brought your mommy and your daddy to a hostage exchange?"

Nate sighed and turned a sheepish glance toward Holly. "We're a close family?"

Holly let loose an amused Elspeth-like cackle and patted his back. "I feel your pain. There's only one other thing that would make this situation worse..."

"The wicked witch is here. Let's get this party started." Elspeth stepped out from her own puddle of shadows, with Harry on her shoulder and Colin the pug at her feet. Holly's grandmother wore all black with a mohawk wig she'd paired with a black camouflage velour jogging suit.

"And there it is."

"Zip it, Death Girl. My dame's presence is a

blessing to all who know her," Colin panted, turning adoring eyes on Elspeth Harrow.

"Blessing. Curse. Same thing." Holly massaged her forehead. Loose cannons and vengeful parents had crashed her plan in a heartbeat.

Harry lifted off Elspeth's shoulder and hovered overhead. "Not much difference when it's a Harrow."

"You're on my list, bird." Elspeth waggled her finger at the mouthy Viking.

"I love you, Sissy. But I didn't sign on for a fight with gods and wicked hags." Samuel crawled backward, all lovey-dovey expressions fleeing in the wake of parental displeasure. He pushed himself to his feet and edged away from Sissy and closer to the bound goddesses. "It was all her idea. I was blinded by emotions."

"Way to celebrate your love, Samuel. I always knew you were a coldhearted worm," Holly sneered. So much for the power of love.

A bright flash lit the night around Nate and a short man with a receding hairline, bald patches, a snappy pinstriped suit, and a black sickle, stepped out into the light. He threw the sickle at Nate. "Thought you might need this, godson."

"Godson?" Holly mouthed at Nate who shrugged.

"It's a family thing."

"No," Sissy wailed. "I had a plan."

"You weren't the only one." Holly inched away from Nate and Hades, closer to Sissy and Samuel.

"And the battle begins. Honor to the warrior who brings the killer down." Harry swooped and dropped an emerald-green water balloon close to Sissy.

Sisyphus used the handle of the sickle to punt the balloon toward the goddesses and a retreating Samuel.

The goddesses yelped and stiffened, as did Samuel. The trio froze, unable to move except for their eyes, which swung frantically from side to side.

Lurching forward, Sissy pushed the frozen trio onto their sides and leapt over them, bolting for the shadows on the other side of the graveyard. Her swift escape was belied by her snowy white curls.

"Don't just stand there, you two." Hades shoved Nate at Holly and nodded at the escaping killer. "Hop off after her." Nate spared Holly a glance before giving chase.

"Man. I had plans for Sissy," Elspeth grumped. Even her mohawk wilted.

Nyx, goddess of the night, edged up next to Elspeth and slid an arm around her shoulder. "I know how you feel. I wanted to flay some skin with my shadow crows, but we really need to let the kids grow up sometime. At least this is what Rebus told me."

"True." Elspeth brightened. "I guess I can always sell the spinster banshee to Death. I'm sure he'd agree. As long as they stay out of my creation cave, that is."

Erebus slapped Elspeth on her bony back, causing her black mohawk to flap over her face. "And there's always future grandkids and great grandkids to torment."

Elspeth beamed, dentures on show. "Torment is one of my favorite words."

TWENTY-ONE

"FYI, cardio is not a core activity of mine." Holly huffed behind Nate, a.k.a. Thanatos, Death personified, as they chased Sissy through the Elysian Fields cemetery.

"Harrows don't normally chase villains, I take it?"

Holly glared at Nate, effortlessly keeping pace, and talking at the same time. "Harrows prefer the villains to come to them."

Soaring overhead, Harry dropped low in front of Sissy, dropping another hex bomb. Exploding smoke, paralyzing vapor, and disappearing ground-causing hex bombs littered the cemetery, but Sissy dodged all.

"She's spry for a white-haired old lady." Nate poured on a burst of speed.

"She's fueled by evil, black doings. She'll probably keep going for miles. I know Elspeth does."

Dropping a large, purple balloon a few paces in front of Sissy, Harry cranked out a left turn and spun away as a large chasm opened up at the killer's feet.

"Curse you." Sissy hissed and spun, Death's cape flaring behind her as she held out the black sickle and pointed it menacingly at the duo.

Holly and Nate slowed to a stop. Thanatos held out his replacement sickle in a similar position as Sissy.

"Do you know what the sickle and cape does, banshee?" Sissy spoke casually as she waved the sickle from side to side. "The sickle reaps the soul and the cloak stores it until they reach their permanent home. Like Tartarus or the Elysian Fields. You can't win, not even Death himself could." Sissy bared her teeth. "But you're welcome to try."

Snickering, Holly slapped her jeans leg. "You're so funny. Have you been practicing that? You were always going to lose. No one wins against a Harrow. Surely, you've heard that?"

"Liar," Sissy shrieked. "I ran rings around you, banshee. You had no clue what was happening until the last minute. Admit it."

Holly blew on her short nails and then rubbed them over her dark-colored shirt. "Whatever gets you through the night, sweet cheeks. Personally, I like hot milk, helps me sleep. Besides, you ran rings around Hades, not me. He really needs to beef up his security. Shameful." She shook her head.

"Sisyphus. You need to turn yourself in. Atone for your crimes. Both old and new." Nate raised his replacement sickle. "Death cannot be bought. It cannot be dodged or beaten."

"Who's wearing Death's cape right now, Thanatos?" Sissy taunted.

"Turn it down, miscreant. You might burst my eardrums. I'm sensitive." Harry dropped low over Sissy's head, raking his talons over her face. "The Viking honors the battle plan," the raven boasted and lifted into the air, but not quite fast enough. Sissy shrieked and swung her sickle, grazing the raven's leg.

The bird stiffened and dropped like a stone to the ground, a few paces away from Sissy, unmoving. Holly screamed, a sudden searing burning in her chest, followed by a sense of loss. She dropped to her knees in front of Harry, stroking his cold, taxidermy feathers. No cursed Viking spirit energizing his taxidermy body. *Nothing.* Tears of rage and loss rolled down Holly's face. She wiped her cheeks on her arm. "The sickle took his soul. He's gone."

"And there's more to come." Sissy smiled maliciously as she raised her sickle above Holly's head.

Joining the fight, Nate countered Sissy's downward stroke with his own sickle. "You'll pay for that, and you'll never touch a hair on the banshee's head." Thanatos pushed Sissy back, trying to protect the still unmoving Holly.

"I'll do more than touch her head. I've already taken out the raven, and the banshee is next. You can watch them both die, knowing there's nothing you can do."

"I wouldn't say that's completely accurate." Elspeth strolled into sight, throwing a tiny, pink ball up and down. "I really need to charge Hades for materials. I just had to subdue Nyx and Erebus because they tried to stop me. *Let the kids handle it, they said.*" Elspeth snorted.

"She killed my cursed Viking." Losing her tight control for once, Holly shrieked. A banshee wail poured from her throat, resonating with raw emotion.

"Now, now, sweetie. We can't have that." Elspeth shook her head. "Only a Harrow can take down one of the family. And as much it pains me to admit it, the raven's family." Elspeth pointed a painted nail at Sisyphus. "And you? You ain't family."

"You're a liar, old hag. You aren't strong enough to handle the Night and the Darkness. No crazy, mouthy witch could take them down."

"Old. Hag. *Old?*" Elspeth roared.

"Aw man." Colin backed away, panting. "You've done it now. She hates ageist people. It's a real trigger."

Amber eyes flashing, Elspeth cackled as forked lightning flashed down, hitting a tree and setting it alight with blue flame. "Never underestimate crazy." Elspeth wound her arm up and let loose her pink ball at Sissy's feet.

"Missed me, hag," Sissy taunted.

"Did I? Did I really?" Elspeth beamed and tapped her foot as if waiting for something to happen.

Taking advantage of the distraction, Sisyphus lunged at Nate. At least, she tried to. But the laces on her boots unraveled, tripping the killer. Sissy flew, as did Death's sickle. The cape wrapped around Sisyphus, trapping her in a cocoon of flapping warmth.

Without warning, Elspeth snapped out a hand, snagging the sickle out of the air, without even breaking a sweat.

A fine mist emanated from the open ball, spreading over Sissy and the others.

Holly tried to wipe the hex mist away from her and Harry, her eyes widening in horror as she realized just what kind of hex Elspeth had exploded. "Tell me that wasn't a bad luck hex?"

"I can tell no lies." Elspeth shrugged. "I just call it collateral damage."

Hades, god of the underworld and annoyed ex-jailer of Sisyphus, flashed next to her and yanked Death's cape off. "You won't need that where you're going." He thrust the cape at Nate. "Try not to lose it again and call your mother once in a while. I can't stand her nagging at me." He placed a hand on Sissy's shoulder, immobilizing her. "I already flashed Mr. Wood to a cell, and you'll be happy to hear the love of your life will be sharing your accommodations for eternity."

Sissy fought Hades' hand, wailing. "No. You can't do that to me. I deserve solitary confinement."

"Personally, I think you're getting exactly what you deserve." Holly waggled her fingers. "Enjoy your afterlife with your eternal love." She sniffed as the god and his prisoner disappeared. "She deserves a heck of a lot more for killing Harry." She stroked Harry's feathers and gathered him up, cradling his empty body gently.

"I owe you, Elspeth Harrow. Don't think I won't

pay up." Nyx flowed into sight, holding the chain of her still bound daughters.

A chuckling Erebus guarded the rear.

"Never get emotional in a take down or leave the kids to deal with their own crap. It's a Harrow rule," Elspeth sneered but then brightened. "As is the traditional victory dance." She flapped her hands and wiggled in her own victory dance.

"Quick, close your eyes," Holly hissed at Nate and followed her own advice. No one needed to see Elspeth's victory twerk. It seared the irises and defiled the mind.

"Too late." Nate's voice rumbled next to the banshee as he slipped a warm hand under her arm and gently helped her stand.

Holly cracked one eye open. "She finished yet?"

"I think she's winding down." Nate whistled to drag his father's horrified gaze away from the twerking, wicked witch. "Dad, can you throw my sickle over here? You can have Hades' replacement." He hefted the sickle the god gave him and pitched it at his father, who snatched it up and replicated his son's action with Death's own sickle. "Thanks, Dad." Nate let out a breath and held his sickle, gently touching it to Harry's chest. "My death is quiet, peaceful. A gentle death is never forced on the unwilling, but death is immovable. Cannot be bribed or forced before the right time. And it is not your time. Harrald, son of Ivor, waken." Nate bellowed the last word, letting it echo around the cemetery, inching into every grave, every headstone, every tree, and blade of grass.

"Keep it down. An old warrior needs sleep." Harry twitched and cracked open a beady eye. "This doesn't look like Valhalla, and you are *not* a Valkyrie."

"That's because it's not your time to die. Not yet." Holly clasped the raven to her chest, her still raw throat clogged with emotion. "You don't get to escape the Harrow family. None of us do."

"Can't. Breathe," Harry gasped out. "And would it kill you to use perfume like the other volvas? It's rancid down here. And hot. Are you running a temperature? I just died. I shouldn't be around germs so soon." The raven wiggled out of Holly's grasp and hopped away, beady eyes gleaming.

"And just like that, everything is back to normal." Holly clapped a hand over her face. Harry might be right. Maybe she had caught a virus from Samuel and Sissy? She touched a gland in her throat. "Is evil catching? I think I'm getting sick."

Erebus let out a bark of laughter. "I'll think you'll

survive, little banshee." He winked at Holly while Nyx still glared and fumed at Elspeth.

Holly sidled up to Nate and teased him. "So, Death, hi. How you doing?"

"I'm not as bad as everyone thinks I am." A faint smile flickered over Nate's lips, but he looked uncertainly at Holly. "Most people don't like having Death around."

"I'm not most people," Holly said in a disgruntled tone.

"No. You're not." Nate travelled light fingers along Holly's cheek. "Death seems to be partial to mouthy Harrows."

Opening and closing her mouth, for once, Holly was speechless. How did an introverted, hypochondriac banshee reply to that?

Elspeth wound down her twerking and pretended to gag. "All this girly stuff makes me want to puke. But one does what one must to make sure great grandchildren are born."

"What?" Holly reared back from Nate, dislodging his hand. "We haven't even had a date yet." She stared in horror at her grandmother.

Elspeth smirked. "Yet..."

TWENTY-TWO

"Can Death die from an overdose of sugar?" Holly's eyes widened as Nate shoveled in another of Lila's *dream big* white chocolate brownies.

Manfully swallowing his mouthful, Nate shot Holly an impish grin. "Some would say Death needs sweetening up."

"I think you're sweet enough." Holly fought her corresponding smile at Nate's flirty words. Who'd have thought having Death hang around could be so much fun?

Elspeth poked her tongue out. "I prefer a low-calorie diet, thanks." She tapped her painted nails on the bakery counter.

"Don't swear. It isn't ladylike." Colin, Elspeth's

pug minion, padded up, strawberry icing spread across his muzzle. "Low-calorie is a bad word."

Harry swept through the bakery, landing on a wooden perch Lila had erected in the corner of the room just for him. "When will Death leave town? His presence irks my rampaging Viking nature."

"Harry," Holly hissed. "Manners." Her cheeks burned red as she traded a heavy glance with Nate. She cleared her throat. "The thing is there's a lot of work in Point Muse for Death." Her voice trailed off as her entire family raised their collective eyebrow. Manning up, Nate continued, "Surprisingly, Point Muse murder counts aren't as high as gentle death rates and since I can work anywhere..." He shrugged. "I've decided to set up shop here in Point Muse. I just need to find an apartment."

Matthew, Lila's reaper boyfriend, whooped. "That's great news, Nate. Welcome to town."

"Settle down, fan boy." Lila rolled her eyes at her boyfriend's excitement.

"I figure there'll be plenty of work, and if there's a lull, I can always help at the funeral home. It's not like Death's squeamish. And I've grown really fond of the town." Nate's eyes cut to Holly's tomato-red face.

"Ha." Elspeth slapped the counter, chortling.

"My plan worked. Maybe I should be a professional matchmaker. I'm three for three granddaughters now." She rubbed her hands gleefully. "Next up, that great-nephew of mine, world domination, and great grandchildren. *Bahahaha.*"

"I am not hooking up and producing great grandkids to satisfy your witchy timetable."

Xandie and Lila agreed with Holly's words, nodding their heads.

Elspeth cackled, and the lights overhead sizzled and popped. The muffled crack of something breaking in the kitchen filtered through the closed door.

"Oh no..." Colin backed out from under a table, his muttered word still audible.

The wicked witch of Point Muse's amber eyes gleamed like cursed jewels as she winked. "You wanna bet..."

The End.

* * *

Want More?

You can sign up for my mailing list. It's for new releases and no spam. Be the first to grab specials, new releases and freebies.

Sign up now.

https://www.kellyethan.com/newsletter

LEAVE A REVIEW

Did you like this book?

Please leave a review for it on Amazon!
Banshee, Death and Disarray

ABOUT THE AUTHOR

Kelly Ethan's world is small town magic, mystery, and mayhem, with plenty of snarky laughs along the way. With an overactive imagination and a love of all things that go bump in the night, it was natural for her to write cozy paranormal mysteries. She loves sarcastic heroines who like to save the day and solve the puzzle. With a busy and chaotic household, writing is her outlet for madness. She lives in Tasmania, Australia and when not writing, can be found plotting her next fictional murder or chasing after the family's ferocious hellhound.

Website:
https://www.kellyethan.com

HOLLY HARROW Point Muse Boxed Set: Books 1-3

The Ghost Vein Mine Cozy Paranormal Mysteries

#1 Ghosts and Gold Dust

#2 Curses and Cold Cases

Non Fiction

Heart and Craft.